MAN

WRIGHT MORRIS

AND

UNIVERSITY OF NEBRASKA PRESS · LINCOLN

BOY

A
BISON
BOOK

Library of Congress Catalog Card Number 51-2263

International Standard Book Number 0-8032-5787-2

First Bison Book printing: January 1974

Most recent printing shown by first digit below:

1   2   3   4   5   6   7   8   9   10

Bison Book edition published by arrangement with the author.

Manufactured in the United States of America

FOR

Louise

If man had beene left *alone* in this *world*, at first, shall I thinke that he would not have *fallen*? If there had beene no *Woman*, would not man have served, to have beene his own *Tempter*?

JOHN DONNE, XXI *Devotion*

MAN
AND
BOY

MR. ORMSBY

In this dream Mr. Ormsby stood in the room
—at the edge of the room where the floor was
bare—and gazed at the figure that seemed to hover
over the yard. This figure had the body of a man
but a crown of bright, exotic plumage—the plumage visible, somehow, in spite of the dented gray
helmet it wore. Long wisps of it appeared at the
side, or shot up, like straw through a leaky pillow,
to make a halo of shining, golden spears. Beneath
the helmet was the face of a bird, a long face, in-
describably solemn, with eyes so pale they were like
openings to the summer sky. The figure was

clothed in a soiled uniform, too big for the boy inside it, and slung over the left arm, casually, was a
gun. On the barrel of the gun Mr. Ormsby could
read—he had read it a thousand times—the word
DAISY, and beneath this the words *1000 Shot*. The
right arm of the figure was extended, and above it
hovered a procession of birds, an endless coming
and going of all the birds he had ever seen. They
formed a whirling cloud about his head, and
seemed to grow like fingers from the extended
hand, but the figure did not speak, nor did the pale
eyes turn to look at Mr. Ormsby; but from the
parted lips came a sound of irresistible charm. A
wooing call, it would seem, for the birds. So they
came and went, thousands of them, and they
looked so lovely and seemed so friendly that Mr.
Ormsby, no bird lover to speak of, put out his hand.
And the moment he did, one of the birds dived at
his head. Not at his hand, no, but his head, and before he could duck or get away, all of these birds,
like a stream of darts, were diving at him. To protect himself he would flail his arms like a man at-

tacked by bees. That woke him up, sooner or later, and sometimes there was sweat all over his body, from either the fright or the violent exercise. There might even be a cloud of bed dust in the air. As his first thought was always for Mother, he would turn on the bed to reassure her, but, strange to relate, the commotion never woke her up. It was uncanny, as Mother was a person who could hear a titmouse enter the bird box—but she never rolled over to question him. He would lie back, his eyes closed, until his heart had stopped pounding, then he would open his eyes and look at the picture on the wall.

In the morning light—it seemed to be the same kind of light in the picture—the boy stood alone on a bomb-pitted rise, a stormy sky and blowing palm trees at his back. Over one arm, casually, he held a gun, and the other he put forward, the palm up, as if making an offering. The palm was empty, but the fingers of the hand were pressed together, so that he seemed to hold, cupped in the palm, a piece of the sky. The face beneath the helmet had no features, but Mr. Ormsby would have known

5

it—the boy, that is—just from the stance. He would have known it by the way the boy held the gun. The boy always held the gun the way women held their arms when their hands were idle, like parts of their body that for the moment were not much use. The boy had two arms and two good legs—right up to the last he had them—but without the gun he gave you the feeling he was not all there. That some vital part, vital limb, that is, had been amputated. He was all thumbs, as his Mother said, and without the gun over his arm he might fall down just walking across the room. It was the gun that made a hero out of him.

He had given the boy a gun because he had never had a gun himself and not because he had wanted him to kill anything. The boy didn't want to kill anything either, and for a while it had worked out pretty well, as the first gun he had wouldn't hurt anything. He shot it at apples, and then shot the b.b.'s over again. The second gun held one thousand shot, and that worked out pretty well too because of the racket the b.b.'s made in the barrel. It was next to impossible to get close to anything. And yet it was that, just *that*, which made a hunter out of him. He had to stalk everything in order to get near it, and after going to all that trouble it was only natural that he took careful aim at it. Even later, when he knew better, the boy never seemed to realize that when he shot and hit something, *that* something was dead. Somehow, that hadn't occurred to him. Mr. Ormsby sometimes wondered if the shot that killed him—for it had been a shot—had come in time to teach him that. That with one shot, so to speak, a man can kill two things. The bird that he is hunting, and perhaps the hunter in himself.

Nobody who knew him had been surprised when the boy ran off and enlisted, nor was anyone surprised when he turned up missing, as they said. He had been missing, some people would say, for a good many years. It seemed only natural to get the official report on it. To Mr. Ormsby it seemed only natural that the boy would turn up something of a hero, though it was a little strange to think of his name being on a boat. The USS *Virgil Ormsby* was not the best name for a destroyer. But it might kill Mother if she knew—in fact, it might kill nearly anybody—what he thought to be the most natural thing of all. Let God strike him dead if he had ever known anything righter, more natural, that is, than that the boy would be killed. It would have been unnatural if he hadn't been. That was something that might prove hard to explain, but it was the one thing that he knew would happen— the boy would find a way, he knew, to fit into the master plan. Mother had a way of getting the best out of everyone.

Mr. Ormsby turned slowly on the bed, careful to keep the coil springs quiet, and as he lowered his feet he reached for his socks on the floor. They were gone. Well, he should have known that. They were gone Sunday mornings and all National holidays. This was not a National holiday, but it was a great day for Mother, and time for him, anyhow, to change his socks. The old pair she had dropped down the laundry chute.

Carrying his shoes, Mr. Ormsby followed the throw rugs to the closet, like a man crossing a swift stream on blocks of ice. The rugs, made of old silk stockings, sometimes slipped on the hardwood floor, so he had learned to pass from corner to corner, where the gap was small. From the closet, by feel—as the chain dragging on the light made a racket—he selected his Sunday pants, and a worn-only-one-time shirt. Once he got it on, Mother wouldn't notice it. Until he got it on she would look at the collar, to see if the wings turned up, or worse yet, hold certain parts of it to her nose. As a test it wasn't really sound, but she relied on it. She would never say "aye," "yes," or "no," but merely hand him back the shirt, or walk down the hall toward the laundry chute with it. The spring lid on the chute came down like a gavel, and meant much the same thing.

As *his* drawer to the bureau was stuck, Mr. Ormsby opened the one above it and reached in behind it to fish out a pair of clean socks. They were in a neat, flat wad, like a pincushion. One reason that he wore his socks too long, once he got them on his feet, was that every clean pair was "done up," as Mother said. It was something of a puzzle just to get it apart. Nine times out of ten he put one of the socks on inside out. It always meant he had to drop everything he had, and take a seat on the stool or the edge of the tub, as he needed both hands as well as one foot at a time to figure it out. There were chairs in the bedroom, but somehow there was never a place to sit.

Although the rest of the house was as neat as a pin, maybe too neat in some respects, the room they seemed to live in, the bedroom, was pretty much of a mess. Mother refused to let Mrs. Dinardo set her foot in it. There was a time Mr. Ormsby had brought the matter up, back when they discussed small things like that, and Mother had said she wanted one room in the house where she could relax. *Let her hair down*—they were the words she used. That had been so extremely unusual for

Mr. Ormsby

Mother—so human as the boy had put it—that they had both been completely taken with it. It had been good to know there was such a room in the house. It was only natural, however, that any room where Mother had her hair down would not be the place for anyone else. Mother's idea of letting her hair down was a long nap in her garden clothes, the cotton gloves on her hands, and the grass-stained shoes at the foot of the bed. Mr. Ormsby let his own hair down at the store, where he had a wood-stove he could put his feet on, and a rolltop desk full of indelible pencils and mail-order blanks. But it had been something of a problem for the boy. The way the boy had taken to the out-of-doors was not so much because he was a great bird lover, or a nature lover, but because he couldn't find a place in the house to sit down. To let *his* hair down, he had to go somewhere else.

They had just redecorated the house that summer—Mr. Ormsby tiptoed down the hall to the bathroom—and Mother had spread newspapers around to protect a few things. There hadn't been a chair in the place—the boy's pants seemed to stick to the ones they had repainted—that hadn't been covered, both the seat and the back, with a newspaper. It was about that time, toward the end of that summer, that Mr. Ormsby took to having his pipe in the basement, and the boy had taken to the great out-of-doors. Otherwise, he might not have even thought of it. But because he had wanted a gun himself, and the boy was alone with no kid around to play with—because of that he had brought home that damn gun. A thousand-shot b.b. gun by the name of DAISY, and five thousand lead b.b.'s in a drawstring bag.

That gun had been a mistake—he began to shave himself in lukewarm water, as when he let it run it banged the pipes, woke Mother up. When the telegram came that the boy had been killed Mother never said a word, no, not a word, but she made it clear, perfectly clear, whose fault it was. He wasn't even drafted, no, that was the hell of it. He wanted to shoot at something or other so badly that he just ran off.

Mr. Ormsby

Mr. Ormsby stopped thinking while he shaved, attentive to the mole at the edge of his mustache, and leaned over the bowl to avoid dropping suds on the rug. There had been a time when he had wondered about an Oriental throw rug in the bathroom, but over the years he had become accustomed to it. As a matter of fact, sometimes he missed it, as when they had overnight guests with young children and Mother remembered, just in time perhaps, to take it up. Without that rug he sometimes felt just a little uneasy, in his own bathroom, and this led him to whistle to himself or turn the cold water on and let it run. If it hadn't been for that he might not have noticed that Mother did the same thing herself, particularly if there was someone in the house. Guests, the iceman, Mrs. Dinardo, or even himself. She would turn on the water and let it run until she was through with the toilet, then she would flush it before she turned the water off. If you happen to have old-fashioned plumbing, and have lived with a person for twenty-three years, you can't help noticing little things

like that. He had got to be a little like that himself.
Since the boy had gone he had got into the habit
of using the toilet in the basement, the one they
had put in, as Mother described it, for the help.

With a folded piece of toilet tissue Mr. Ormsby
wiped off the rim of the bowl, then stepped back
to see if he had spilled anything. There was an ant
crossing the floor—a rainy summer always brought
them in—and he stooped over and let the ant crawl
on the back of his hand. Then he walked to the
window, unhooked the screen, and blew the little
fellow into the back yard. After he did this he remembered that *now* they were killing ants. They
had become a Victory Garden pest. But for a little
more than twenty years Mother had trained him
not to kill *anything*, and with the boy around that
was one rule that he didn't break. Mother was a
girl of the old school—which made life a little
harder in some ways, but in other ways where in
the world would you find a woman to match? It
was openly admitted—see that feature editorial in
the *Bulletin* just three months ago—that Mother

had, singlehanded, saved a good part of the nation for the quail. And the quail, as she put it, would save that much of the nation for her.

With his socks on, but carrying his shoes—"The hour I love," Mother had said, "is the hour before arising"—Mr. Ormsby left the bathroom and tiptoed down the stairs. There was no reason, as he had explained to Mother the spring they were married, why she should get up when he could just as well get breakfast for himself. He had made that suggestion at a time when he was looking forward to the baby, and Mother had been, that first year, a pretty frail girl. She needed, as he had said, to preserve her strength. The truth was that he needed to preserve his own, as he had a lot of early morning work at the store, and one of Mother's breakfasts might take two or three hours. It always took half the dishes around the place. Every one of these dishes had to be soaked for fifteen minutes in boiling water, washed with a cloth, and then carefully rinsed three times. And when it came to dishes,

Mother wouldn't be rushed. Ever since Mrs. Dinardo had told her about Mr. Dinardo's case of trench mouth, pretty much in detail, Mother washed and scoured the silver herself. That took about forty minutes, and she liked to superintend his wiping it.

If he got away early he had time, in the late afternoon, to do the shopping, and this got him home near the middle of Mother's nap. While she dressed and had her bath, he would prepare the meat. He had found he had a flair for meat at the time when Mother, who liked to eat it, found it made her nearly sick to handle it in the bloody stage. He had gone from meat to vegetables, easily. If he didn't have a flair, he could still keep an eye on them while they were cooking, something Mother, with her mind full of things, found it hard to do. She didn't have a sense of time, which he seemed to, and it always seemed to be around supper that important people tried to get her on the telephone. Calls from Washington might go on for half an hour. There was always something Mother was trying to push through the House. The phrase troubled Mr. Ormsby, hard to say why. It was nearly always something worth while—housing for the poor, or more refuge for the quail—but he often had the feeling that the opposition was being pushed around. That never proved to be true, as Mother was nearly always singlehanded, and fighting for things that very few people seemed to care much about. It had made her, as everybody knew, a great force in the state. She was nearly always alone, but Mr. Ormsby could never get over the feeling, come what might, that the opposition was scared to death. Sooner or later, she would push it through the House.

There had been a year—at the foot of the stairs Mr. Ormsby peered into the living-room—when Mother had made several marvelous meringue pies. That had been before the boy had taken up with the gun. But feeling as she did about the gun—and she let them know how she felt about it—she refused to slave, as she said, in the kitchen for people like that. She always spoke to them as *they*—or as *you* plural—from the day he had given the boy that gun. When she called for something *they* both would answer, and though the boy had been gone three years Mr. Ormsby still felt him there, right beside him, when Mother said *you*.

He felt the same way about the living-room. The boy was gone, the boy was dead, but he could never enter the room without pausing, like a stranger, to peer into it. One morning he had found the boy, with all of his filthy outdoor clothes on, sprawled out asleep where Mother had forbidden him to sit. It had given him quite a shock, as the boy lay asleep *under* the newspapers that Mother had spread out to protect the new cushions. His feet stuck out, like a tramp asleep in a park. Naturally, he should have punished the boy—at the very least have made him get up—but he had tip-toed by as if Mother lay there asleep. His mouth had opened, but he hadn't said a word. Part of that was probably the shock of it, but the reason he hadn't called to him was that the boy for some time had had no name. He had one, of course, but they had stopped using it. Virgil was all right for a baby, or a little boy with a head of dark curls, but it was nothing a father could call his son. There had been one week he had called him Son—but he had given up doing that, as the boy was always startled to learn who *that* was. He would look around the room to see who else was there. It was either Virgil or nothing, as Mother had carefully explained to them both that she had not named him Virgil for his father to call him something else. So it had been nothing—that is to say, he called him Virgil when speaking to Mother, but in his own mind he always referred to him as the Boy.

From the table beside the piano Mr. Ormsby picked up his watch, his car keys, and about ninety cents in change. As these things often fell out of his pockets when he took his pants off in the bedroom, Mother had suggested that he empty his pockets downstairs. Beneath his leather wallet were two aspirin tablets, the official invitation to the USS *Ormsby*, and a note in Mother's hand reading: *Remember icebox pan.*

It was Mother's habit, over the years, to jot the important things down in a note, but it had reached the point where there were notes all over the house. She wrote a note instead of speaking to him. Mother found it a very sensible system, but it had the effect, over the years, of cutting down on what little they had to say. There were days when they seldom exchanged a word. Sometimes Mother would get up from the table and search high and low for a pencil, finally borrow his own, and then sit down and write him a note. It was one of the things—the good things—she was apt to carry too far.

Take the icebox pan, for instance. It might be hard to explain to some people why a woman like Mother, so advanced in her thinking, still had an icebox with a drip pan underneath. Mr. Ormsby sold electric iceboxes himself—he tried to, that is— and Mother might have agreed, just for business reasons, to use one of them in the house. It was not that Mother was old-fashioned—no, nothing like that—it was just that she refused to buy anything but the best. Right up until Pearl Harbor there had been so many new improvements, and new models, that she hadn't been able, as she said, to honestly make up her mind. Nor did she think the last word on the subject had been said. She couldn't make up her mind, for instance, whether the gas type was worth the extra money, or whether those boxes with all the moving parts really did wear out. And after Pearl Harbor it was all out of the question— for a woman like Mother—so the icebox pan would have to be remembered for several more years.

Spreading a newspaper on the floor, Mr. Ormsby got down on his knees, lifted the wooden diaper, and carefully withdrew the pan. It was full to the lip, and at the bump in the linoleum it spilled. He felt it soak the bottom of his sleeve, and then both knees. He spilled a little more getting up with it, a little more again at the screen, and in his haste to miss the porch he poured most of it into the lidless garbage-pail. Scallions, wads of Kleenex, and other tidbits floated to the top. He stood a moment speculating whether Mother would notice this, decided that she would, and went off with the pail behind the garage. There he poured off the water, brought the rest of the garbage back to the house. Mother kept an eye on every piece of garbage for her compost pit. As he crossed the yard he saw two birds fighting over a piece of suet, one of the birds a small woodpecker of some kind. Mother had told him, time and again, just which pecker it was, but somehow he could never remember it. He liked birds—that is to say he didn't have anything against them; or hadn't, anyhow, until he was supposed to remember their names. It was because of birds that he had met Mother—won her, as a matter of fact— because he was the one who used to feed them in the park. He had always liked birds—he had just assumed that they had enough sense to go about their own business, until the summer Mother got him to spying on them. One morning he had stood at the kitchen window and watched one of them worm the yard just to be worming—not eating a single one of them. The first two or three worms had been interesting—he had made a mental note of it for Mother—but after that he had the feeling that the bird was just a plain damn fool. He was just another one of these modern gadgets put out by some firm for worming your yard, and like most gadgets he didn't have sense enough to stop. What seemed very sweet about hauling out one worm drove a man crazy on the tenth, with all the other nine worms lying there in the yard. He had gone out himself and buried five or six of them.

The same week Mother pointed out a robin with one of his pipe cleaners in his beak, which she said it was going to put in its nest. A busy woman, Mother didn't have time to wait and see what it did with it, or tried to do with it for the next two weeks. For two weeks that fool robin had tried to build a nest where no bird in its right mind would build anything. It would get so far, then all the grass and the string and the pipe cleaner would tumble down—and then it would start all over again. That went on for two weeks, and naturally he didn't tell Mother, as something like that would have just made her sick. He wasn't Mother, but he hadn't felt any too well himself. It was on his mind at night, and sometimes kept him from getting to sleep. After a week or so he had to stop watching, and he even left the house by the front door, something he seldom did, rather than see that fool pipe cleaner again. As for that robin, he hoped she cracked up. It made him nearly sick to think what the male robin must think of her. Mother simply didn't have the time to watch birds long enough to see something like that, and though he seemed to have the time, he didn't have the temperament.

On his knees again, facing the icebox, Mr. Ormsby wiped up the water he had spilled, and then returned the pan to the left-hand corner, under the drip. Kneeling there, he wiped up the dirt he had tracked in. The linoleum was blue, with a white and gray speckle, but Mr. Ormsby saw it so seldom he was never sure just what the color was. Six days a week the kitchen floor was covered with newspapers. Saturday night they were taken up, and the floor remained uncovered until Sunday noon, at which time he came back from town with the Sunday *New York Times* and the *Bulletin*. Mr. Ormsby had a glance at the papers in the drugstore, along with a cup or two of coffee, as it was usually his last chance for a look at parts of them. Once he got them home, they were spread out on the kitchen floor. Mother liked to have the floor newly covered before they got around to the Sunday dinner, as it was apt to be the messiest meal of the week. Grease was meant for axles, she liked to say, and not linoleum.

The truth was—it occurred to Mr. Ormsby as he was kneeling there, reading—that they both did most of their reading with the papers spread out on the floor. They missed a good deal that way, but they didn't miss *everything*. He nearly always missed the comics, as Mother couldn't stand to see them face up on the floor, and most continued stories were pretty difficult to track down. But the headlines were usually there at the foot of the stairs. That was why Mother—it had taken him two, maybe three or four, years to catch on to it—liked to have a little snack, with her second cup of coffee, sitting there. Sitting down that low she could read most of the fine print as well.

He stood up—all that bending for the drip pan nearly always stirred up his bowels—and measured out a pint of water, a little more than a pint, in the enamel saucepan. He added salt, and put the pan over a medium flame. From the raincoat on the cellar door he removed his pipe and four or five matches, and then walked down the cellar stairs to the basement, made a turn to the left. Standing there in the cool darkness he lit his pipe. Then he dipped his head, bending low, to pass beneath a sagging line of wash, and with one hand out before him like a sleepwalker, he entered the closet.

The basement toilet had been put in to accommodate the help, who had to use something, and

Mr. Ormsby

Mother wouldn't have them on her Oriental rug. But until the day he dropped some money on the floor, and had to strike a match, inside, to look for it, Mr. Ormsby hadn't noticed just what kind of a stool it was. Mother had picked it up, as she had told him, second-hand. There was no use, as she had pointed out, why she should buy anything new or fancy for a place that was meant to be in the dark. He hadn't pushed the matter, and she hadn't offered more than that. What he saw was very old, with a chain pull, and operated on a principle that was very effective, but invariably produced quite a splash. The boy had named it the Ormsby Falls. That described it pretty well, it was constructed on that principle, and in spite of the splash they both preferred it to the one upstairs. This was a hard thing to explain, as the seat was pretty cold over the winter; but it was private like no other room in the house. The first time the boy had turned up missing, he had been there. It was that time when the boy had said—when his father nearly stepped on him—"*Et tu, Brutus*," and sat

there blowing through his nose. Laughing so hard
Mr. Ormsby thought he might be sick. Like everything the boy said there had been two or three
ways to take it, and there in the dark Mr. Ormsby
couldn't see his face. He had just stood there, not
knowing what to say. Then the boy stopped
laughing and said: "You think we ought to make
one flush do, Pop?" and Mr. Ormsby had had to
brace himself on the door. To be called Pop had
made him so weak he couldn't speak, his legs felt
hollow, and when he got himself back to the stairs
he had to sit down. Just as he had never had a name
for the boy, the boy had never had a name for him
—one, that is, that Mother would permit him to
use. And of all the names she couldn't stand, Pop
was the worst. Mr. Ormsby didn't like it either, he
thought it just a vulgar common name, a comic
name used by smart alecks to flatter old men. He
agreed with her completely—until he heard the
word in the boy's mouth. It was hard to believe a
common word like that could mean what it did.
Nothing more had been said, ever, but it remained

their most important conversation—so important that they were both afraid to improve on it. Only later, hours later, did he remember the rest of the boy's sentence, that it wasn't very proper, and implied a very strange state of mind. But he had better sense than to bring the matter up. When you know what you'll find under rocks you don't have to go around turning them over.

When the telegram came—and when he knew, knew without a doubt, what he would find in it— he had put it in his pocket and come downstairs to open it. There in the dark he had struck a match, read what it said. The match had filled the cell with light, and when he looked up from the telegram he saw—he couldn't help seeing—small piles of canned goods in the space beneath the stairs. Several dozen cans of tunafish and salmon, among other things. As Mr. Ormsby was the man who had the ration points—they were *pinned* to his coat, on the inside pocket—there was only one place that Mother could have obtained such things. It had been a greater shock than the telegram—that was the honest-to-God truth—and anyone who knew Mother, really knew her, would have felt the same. Cultures died, wars came and went, young men gave their lives for their country, but Mother did *not* stash away black market tunafish. It was unthinkable, but there it was—and there were more cans piled on top of the water closet, tins of pineapple, crabmeat, liver paste, and Argentine beef. He had been stunned, the match had burned down and blackened the nails on two fingers, and then he had nearly killed himself when he stepped off the stool. He had forgotten that he had climbed up there to peek.

Later in the day—after he had sent flowers to ease the terrible blow for Mother—it occurred to him how such a thing must have happened. Mother knew hundreds of influential people, top people in all the walks of life, and such people were always giving her things. They had been, up until the war that is. Then it had stopped—or rather it had gone underground. Around Christmas he had often wondered about it. Rather than turn these offerings

down and needlessly alienate some very fine people, Mother had managed, worked out, that is, the
stow-away plan. It was, in a way, typical of her.
While the war was on she had refused to serve the
food, or profiteer in any way, and at the same time
she didn't alienate people foolishly. It was the way
she had pushed the quail bill through the House.

Mr. Ormsby struck another match to see if everything was all right—hastily blew it out when he
saw that the pineapple pile had increased. It *had*
been an odd thing, certainly, and what Mother
would call a coincidence, that he had discovered
the pirate's horde with the same match he had read
the telegram by. One match had done for both of
them. And when this match went out, they remained buried in the same spot. The same darkness
fell about both of them. Mr. Ormsby paused to reflect on this, to ponder again its hidden meaning,
but he was distracted by a bubbling sound at the
top of the stairs. The egg water was boiling. Holding his pants with one hand, he ran for the stairs.

As the water had boiled down considerably he

added half a cup, wiped the steam from the face of the stove clock. Seven thirty. He checked his own watch. As it would be a hard day for Mother —naming a boat *sounded* complicated—he would give her eight or ten minutes more. If a bottle had to be broken, it would take strength. He took two egg cups from the cupboard, set them on powder-blue pottery saucers, and the saucers on ivory-white plates. On one side of the plates he put a knife, on the other a spoon. Then he turned, out of habit, and opened the icebox door.

As he put in his head—it was dark inside, and about the temperature of a cave—Mr. Ormsby checked his breathing, closed his eyes. What had been dying for some time was now dead. He leaned back, inhaled deeply, leaned in again. The floor of the icebox was covered with assorted jars, deep and shallow saucers, and Mason-jar lids containing a spoonful of something. Some of the jars were covered with transparent hoods, some with saucers, inverted cups, and paper snapped down with a rubber band. Something seemed to be growing, thriving, in all of them. From the outside, peering in, no nose could tell you which was the culprit, but it could tell you, beyond doubt, that something was dead. Mr. Ormsby seated himself on the floor. He began at the front, and worked slowly toward the back. As he had done this many times before, he got well into the problem, near the middle, that is, before troubling to sniff at anything. Otherwise, he might not last it out. A mayonnaise jar that might have been carrots—it was hard to tell without probing—was now a furry marvel of green mold. Not unlike the glass bells— terrariums, Mother called them—that were offered for sale in the windows of florist shops. It smelled only mildly, however, and Mr. Ormsby reflected that this was probably penicillin, the life-giver. A spoonful of cabbage—it had been two or three months since they had had cabbage—had a powerful stench but was still not the odor he had in mind. He found two more jars of mold, and the one with the lid on tight he ignored, as the glass had a frosted look and the top of the heavy lid bulged. It would have to be buried as it was, not looked into. The culprit, however, was not in a jar at all, but in an open saucer covering a green cherry tart. Part of an egg—Mr. Ormsby had beaten the white himself. He placed this saucer in the sink, then he returned all of the jars to the icebox, in their proper order, except for the one with the bulging lid. When they reached that stage he took them out. He wasn't pulling any wool over Mother's eyes, as she knew every jar and smell in the box, but she had learned that it was wise to accept some things. A jar with a tight, bulging lid was one of them.

When the boy had been just a little shaver, maybe six or seven years old, he had once walked in on one of Mother's parties, with a jar in his hands. He had walked around the room with it, showing it to Mother's guests. The glass was foggy, but it wasn't hard to see the explosive inside. Any other woman would have died, any *mother*, certainly, would have died on the spot, but Mother just sat there with a charming smile on her face. She didn't speak to him, or get up and hustle him out. By her not saying a word every woman in the room got the impression that this was something the boy was growing for himself. One of his nature studies, and that she was *very* proud of him. There was simply no accounting for the way Mother could turn a blow like that, but it always made him think of what Mrs. Dinardo said. Mrs. Dinardo had known Mother right from the first. "She'll surprise you, Mr. Ormsby," she said. And that was that. Even after twenty years there was no disputing *that*.

With the puffy lidded jar in his hands Mr. Ormsby turned to look at the clock, saw that it was now seven thirty-eight. He stood there, his eyes lidded, calculating the amount of time he would need to dig the hole, bury the jar, and get back to the house. Hearing the clink of milk bottles he opened his eyes and saw Peter Ludlow, the milkman, staring at him over the sweating tops of two quarts of milk. On Peter Ludlow's simple face was the expression of a man who had seen strange things. Mr. Ormsby managed to wag the jar of mold at him. Peter Ludlow backed away, then he was back—his hand was back at the window—with a jar of cottage cheese that he had forgotten to leave with the milk. The hand placed the jar on the sill, then was gone. Mr. Ormsby stood there until he heard the clop-clop-clop of General, the milk horse, and the sound of empty bottles as Mr. Ludlow hurried away. From afar, faint but persistent, he heard the Erskine's alarm clock ring. A quarter to eight. The Ormsby clock was three minutes slow. He returned the jar of mold to the icebox, fanned the door several times to ventilate it, then opened the kitchen door to the stairwell, put in his head.

"Ohhhh Mother!" he called, and waited for her to rap on the floor.

MOTHER

Rapping her mule heels on the floor she said: "Modern man is obsolete, Mrs. Dinardo," and rose from the bed to peer at the bird box in the window seat. A purple grackle, *Quiscalus quiscula*, peered back at her. He gave her eye for eye, and his yellow hatpin eye did not blink. Folding the loose flaps of her robe around her, Mother drew it closed at the knees and throat, then closed her eyes as she passed between the mirrors to the closet door. In the darkness she felt about for her corset, then overhead for the dangling cord, gave it a pull, and in a firm voice declared: *"Fiat lux."*

Light having been made, dim light, Mother opened her eyes.

As the light bulb hung in the attic, behind a flowered shower curtain, the closet remained in a rosy, offstage, twilight zone. It was not light, but it was all Mother wanted to see. Seated on the steps she trimmed her toenails with Mr. Ormsby's pearl-handled knife, the one he had been missing, along with the chain, for several years. The blade was not so good any more, and may have aggravated three ingrown toenails, but Mother preferred it to the secret weapon of the Home. *Even more than the battlefield, Mrs. Dinardo, the most dangerous place in the world, thanks to scissors, bathtubs, and general failure to dry between toes.*

From the closet door she removed her kimono, cream-colored with a dragon before Pearl Harbor —after Pearl Harbor without the dragon and deep chocolate brown. On the board that did not squeak she crossed the hall, carrying her mules, and entered the bathroom, where she turned on the hot-water tap before locking the door. As the pipes began to pound she removed from the roll of toilet paper three double sheets, and between these sheets she blew her nose. First the right nostril, careful to keep both of the nostrils open, then the left, with particular attention to the right. That done, she turned the hot water off, let the pounding die down. As there was still a noise in the pipes she opened the lid to the laundry chute, put in her head, and partially lidded her eyes. The sound of the basement toilet rose up to her. Her head still in the chute she said: "Oh, Warren."

"Yes, Mother," he answered, then he added: "I'll fix that right away." As she heard his feet on the basement stairs she let the lid snap down on the chute.

Facing the mirror, and seeing in the mirror her mouth spread wide by the index fingers, she examined the teeth, filled and unfilled, and the wax-colored gums. *My dear Mrs. Bailey,* she thought, then she removed the fingers from her mouth to say, *there is no pyorrhea among the Indians,* and moistened the first finger of her right hand, mas-

saged her gums. Removing the cap from the bottle
of Air-Wick, she took a faint whiff, up each nostril, then walked the bottle to the four corners of
the room. In the window corner she paused to
watch Mr. Ormsby, a garden fork in his hand,
crawl through the rhododendron at the back side
of the garage. He wore his rubber raincoat, and
the flap concealed something. She knew. She let
him get to the back of the yard, then she hammered
with her brush on the bathtub plumbing until the
sound, like the pipes of an organ, seemed to vibrate
the house. She stopped hammering to watch him
run for the house. She was in the bedroom, at the
back of the closet, seated among the toenail clip-
pings, when she heard him skid on the papers near
the stove. He fell, then he got up and opened the
door.

"Mother—?" he said.

"Is it blue or brown for Navy, Warren?"

In the quiet she could hear water somewhere.

"Do I hear water running?" she said.

"Just boiling, Mother."

Mother

"Oh Warren—"

"Yes, Mother—"

"Is it blue or brown for Navy?"

"It's blue, Mother," he answered. "For the Navy it's blue."

MR. ORMSBY

WHEN he heard Mother's feet on the stairs Mr. Ormsby cracked her soft-boiled eggs and spooned them carefully into the heated cup. He heard her reach the landing, open the door, but when she failed to say "Bon jour, Warren," her customary greeting, he turned toward her with the eggshells in his hand. Mother stood on the landing, her left hand half-upraised, in an attitude of blessing, and the index finger of her right hand pressed to her lips. As he knew what that meant, Mr. Ormsby turned to the kitchen window, scanned the chicken-wire bird box, then looked beyond it at the yard.

He saw nothing. But he stood hushed as a man who did.

"Blackbird—?" he said, tentatively, as the yard was often full of *black*birds.

"Listen for the *zeeeeeee*—" Mother said, and perhaps she heard it, for she added: "*Bombycilla cedrorum*," and leaned over the kitchen stove. Watermelon seeds, spread out in a pan lid, were drying over the lighter flame. Mother didn't care for melons, but some birds liked the seeds. "Blackbird—" she said, getting back to where he had interrupted, "any bird is a blackbird if the males are largely, or entirely black."

Well, he knew that, but it didn't seem to help him much. Besides, talk about male and female birds troubled him. Although Mother was a girl of the old school she would never hesitate, *anywhere*, to speak right out about male and female birds. A cow was a cow, a bull was a bull, but to Mr. Ormsby a bird was a bird. To change the subject he said: "Mother, you like your toast dark?"

"Among the birdfolk," Mother said, "the menfolk, so to speak, wear the feathers. The female has more serious work to do."

Mother made this observation from behind the kitchen cabinet. She had her best thoughts, seemed to do her best thinking, *behind* something. Very rarely she spoke them, most of the time she wrote them down on a pad. They sometimes had something like a conversation between the first and the second floors, but it stopped the moment one of them came into view. It also stopped, by and large, when Mother made a sharp observation—such as the one she was nationally famous for. Before the Friends of the Quail, a national organization, she had given a talk she called "Consider the Lilies," with special reference to the fact that they toiled not, neither did they spin. What she had in mind, as she pointed out, was not lilies but birds—male birds, of course, in particular. Requests for reprints of this speech were still pouring in. Small boys wrote in to say that they were now shooting only male birds. That was carrying it further than she wanted to go, but it was characteristic of Mother, just as she always seemed to be saying more than she said. He had never seen nor heard of a woman with a greater store of pithy sayings, though it sometimes took a little reflection to figure them out. The saying was plain enough, but Mother always managed to use it, like she did the lilies, in a very original way. It gave what was generally described as depth to everything she said.

Mr. Ormsby waited for her to continue—one good thought often led to another—but the far side of the cabinet was quieter than usual. He faced toward the window, thinking it must be another bird.

"Robin makes nest in street car—" Mother began, in the careful voice she reserved for reading, but a little strained as the paper she read was on the floor. "Eggs leave in morning—" she continued, "return to Mother at night. Conductor in quandary as to whether bird in egg is full fare."

Putting down the eggshells, Mr. Ormsby walked into the living-room, found the scissors, then came back and snipped the article out. He put it in the

Indian bowl on top of the cabinet. Mother had moved on to Walter Lippmann, which she read aloud in snatches, with reference to the passages that she would later underline. As he had learned, this performance was not for him. Mother read some things aloud to impress them, as she said, on her own mind. There was a pause, she took a spoonful of her egg, and as he poured her cup of coffee she said:

"Put a dozen fresh eggs in a bag, Warren, she never sees a fresh egg."

"She—?" he said.

"Mrs. Dinardo," Mother said.

That was the way her mind worked, all over the place in one cup of coffee, Walter Lippmann one moment, Mrs. Myrtle Dinardo the next. The eggs on his mind, Mr. Ormsby said: "If she's not going to have a spare room, Mother—"

"She has a house full of rooms," Mother said.

"Comparatively speaking—" Mr. Ormsby said, "her new quarters are considerably larger—" he stopped to reflect on the Dinardo family in the Race Street rooms. Nine Dinardos—now that three were in the war—in two and one-half rooms. Then Mr. Dinardo got a fine job in the Navy Yard, somewhere in Brooklyn, and Mrs. Dinardo had found a flat on 116th street. She had asked Mother to come and visit her. Mother had picked up the impression —she seemed to have trouble with Mrs. Dinardo's letters—that in her new place she had room for all of them. "As I remember—" Mr. Ormsby said, and left the kitchen to look for the letter.

"Under D in the telephone book," Mother called. He found the letter under D—Mother never wrote, she telephoned, and used the telephone book as a letter-filing case.

Returning with the letter, he began: " 'Dear Mrs. Ormsby—' "

"Cowbird—" Mother interrupted, "*Molothrus ater*. Go on."

" 'Dear Mrs. Ormsby—' " he said again, then stopped to scan the page, as Mrs. Dinardo had a very unusual style. " 'I received your letter and I sure was glad to know that you are both well and think of me often and I often think of you too—' "

47

It went on, but he stopped there to get his breath.

"Is that all?" Mother said.

" 'Well, Mrs. Ormsby—' " he continued, " 'I have more rooms all over the place and never know whether one of them or how many is empty at once. But come to See me I will have Something if you need Something.' " Mrs. Dinardo, for some reason, always liked to make a capital S, which made it a little harder to scan her style. " 'We are both well—' " he went on, " 'and he is Still in the Navy Yard. My I do wish the War is over it is So long. Do come and See us when you put your name on the boat. Mrs. Ormsby, wouldn't a Street suit you better than a boat? If you're going to put your name on Something why not a Street? Here in my hand is news of a boat just Sunk what is wrong with a Street? Well, we have the river here so near and it is nice. If you don't find Something you can leave it to me to find Something. Love, Mrs. Myrtle Dinardo.' "

It was quite a letter to get from a woman that Mother had known, known Mother, that is, for something better than twenty years. Mrs. Dinardo, had been brought in to nurse the boy. Something in Mother's milk, Dr. Paige had said, when it was plain as the nose on your face that it was nothing in the milk, but something in the boy. He just refused, plain refused, to nurse with her. The way the little rascal would look at her, making a face like the milk was sour, and then the way he would gurgle when Mrs. Dinardo would scoop him up. For a year she was there every day in the week, listening to Mother talk about birds and flowers while she ate all of the wonderful things that Mother cooked. Mrs. Dinardo had been hired to cook, as well as sit around and nurse the boy, but so far as he knew she never once put a hand to the stove. Mother spent the mornings cooking something special for her lunch.

Turning from the window Mother said: "What does she say?"

"What she means to say—" Mr. Ormsby began—

"I'll telephone," Mother said, and picked up her

egg cup, her spoon, and her saucer, and headed for the sink. Mr. Ormsby cut in behind the cupboard to head her off. If she once got to the sink, she might be there for an hour.

"Now let me take care of that, Mother—" he said, but being as she often was when her mind was busy, preoccupied that is, she didn't seem to see him standing there. She walked right past him and took her stand at the sink. With one hand—with the other she held her bathrobe close about her—she let the water slowly run into the large dishpan. "Mother—" he said, "now you telephone. You better telephone while you're sure to get her."

"Cold water," Mother said matter-of-factly, "cold water for eggs."

Long ago, long, long ago, Mr. Ormsby had learned the unwisdom of discussing with Mother the problem of washing egg. He took the dish-towel from the rack, folded it over his arm. He stood there while Mother went about the money-saving business of trying to make suds with a little piece of soap in a wire cage. The soap was very old, about the size of a button, and nothing like suds ever appeared, but the thrashing in the water stirred up a few bubbles that looked like soap. To meet this problem Mr. Ormsby kept, on top of the radiator under the sink, a paper bag full of fine powdered soap. Sooner or later, he would get his hand into it. From there to the dishpan was a simple step. "You see—?" Mother would say, as the water began to suds, and hold up the stale button of soap for him to admire. He always did. It was getting to be something he believed in himself.

"My own opinion—" Mr. Ormsby began, his mind still on the Dinardo business, but he stopped when Mother raised her hand. There were times when she looked exactly like the girl in the *Song of the Lark*. Like that girl, she was listening, but it was hard to tell if what Mother heard was more leaky plumbing, a thought coming on, or some rare bird. They stood quiet, and Mr. Ormsby listened to the stove clock, said to be silent, but nothing had been said about the low-keyed hum, like a time bomb.

"*Hylo*—something *mustelina*—" Mother said, and

dropped the wire cage, headed for the window. As she did, Mr. Ormsby got his hand into the bag of powdered soap. "Except for the nightingale," Mother said, her head in the window looking for it, "the most popular of European songbirds."

"Very pretty," Mr. Ormsby said, and in the distraction of the moment he had time to dip his hand in the water, work up a suds.

"Hark!" Mother said, and Mr. Ormsby stilled the hand he held in the water, and heard again, like the rumblings of his stomach, the ominous whirring of the clock.

While Mr. Ormsby washed the dishes Mother put out some fresh suet for the birds and some Pepperidge Farm whole wheat bread for the squirrels. It had got so the squirrels wouldn't touch anything else. It was either Pepperidge Farm or nothing, and as in most cases it was nothing, Mother saw to it that they got their Pepperidge Farm. As he finished wiping the silver Mother came in with some flowers for Mrs. Dinardo, and arranged them, for a moment, in a tall glass.

"According to her letter—" Mr. Ormsby began—

"Warren," she said, "your hands are dripping."

Mr. Ormsby put his hands over the sink and said: "If we're going to be met at the Pennsylvania station—if we're going to be met by Commander Sudcliffe—I don't see how we're going to give her any bouquet. I don't see just how we're going to deliver a dozen fresh eggs."

"I know that neighborhood," Mother said. "There isn't a fresh egg anywhere in it."

"We go from the station to the boat," said Mr. Ormsby, "and as I understand, the boat is over in Brooklyn. To get to Brooklyn you don't go near 116th street."

On the wall beside the icebox was a pad of paper with a blue pencil dangling on a string. On the top sheet of the pad Mother had already written *Ars longa, vita brevis*, but that had been last night and she had forgotten why. She stood there, the pencil point in her mouth, reflecting on it.

"My own opinion is—" Mr. Ormsby said, "that we name the boat and then hustle back home. Right now it's pretty hard to find a room in New York."

"Milkman—" Mother said, tearing off the top sheet and using a clean one. "Milkman—Gone for 2 days. Please leave no milk."

In very jovial tones Mr. Ormsby said: "I'll bet we're right back here before dark, Mother." And that was *all* he said. That was every last word of it. All he wanted to do, in fact, all he did, was to try and call Mother's attention to the fact that Mrs. Dinardo was not any too sure about rooms. And that 116th street, down near the river, was not exactly on the route. That was all he said, but in the middle of her note, right at the end of the word "days," she dropped the pencil, took a tuck in her bathrobe, and headed for the stairs. He knew. He knew what the tuck in that bathrobe meant. Mother never argued, she never raised her voice, she merely took a tuck in whatever she was wearing and then

54

a week might pass before she spoke to anyone. The silent treatment left no room for argument. From the top of the stairs, she said, in a voice she reserved for peddlers:

"Would you tell Commander Sudcliffe, Mr. Ormsby, that Mrs. Ormsby has decided to remain at home? She's getting old, you know, and there are soooo many things she doesn't seem to know." She let that sink in, then she added: "After all, it's *your* name on the boat, Mr. Ormsby. It doesn't matter whose mother's son it is, you know. It's the name on the boat."

So gently that he couldn't hear the latch, she closed the door. But he heard the key. She wanted him to hear the key turn in the lock. In the quiet Mr. Ormsby heard his swollen red hands drip water on the floor.

Although he had been through this a thousand times—into it, that is, he had never been through it—he was never ready for it, somehow it always took him by surprise. And after all of these times it never left him anything at all but sick. He went into the front room, where it was dark, and let himself drop down before he remembered—but he remembered the moment his bottom crumpled the papers in the chair. He got up and looked around the room for a place to sit down. In the fireplace corner, behind the rack that held the unabridged dictionary, he found the Pennsylvania Dutch authentic milk stool, sat down on it. It brought his knees up so he could rest his head and arms on them. Ordinarily he could get up and leave the house and after four or five days it might blow over, but in all his life—their life, that is—there had been nothing like this. The Government of the United States was banking on her. Also banking on her—somewhere in Brooklyn—was a boat. At the thought of it he got up from the stool and walked to the table where the correspondence, eight months of it, was on display chronologically. There it all was, about twenty pages of it, *his* correspondence in a sense, as he had taken every piece of it down to the office, answered it there. Then brought home the letter he had written, for Mother to sign. He picked up the first:

NAVY DEPARTMENT

BUREAU OF NAVAL PERSONNEL

Mrs. Violet Ames Ormsby

Bel Air, Pa.

My dear Mrs. Ormsby:

As he knew it by heart, he put it down, picked up the one from the Secretary of the Navy.

THE SECRETARY OF THE NAVY

WASHINGTON

Mrs. Violet Ames Ormsby

Bel Air, Pa.

My dear Mrs. Ormsby:

He glanced at the signature, the *personal* signature of the Secretary of the Navy, then he put that letter down and thumbed ahead several months.

OFFICE OF THE SUPERINTENDENT OF SHIPBUILDING

U. S. NAVY

Mrs. Violet Ames Ormsby
Bel Air, Pa.

My dear Mrs. Ormsby:

That letter described what boat it would be, about when it would be ready for launching, and was followed by a letter from the builders themselves.

FEDERAL SHIPBUILDING AND DRYDOCK CO.

KEARNEY, N. J.

Mrs. Violet Ames Ormsby
Bel Air, Pa.

My dear Mrs. Ormsby:

There they all were—in a handstitched folder with cellophane sheets so that one could read them—along with the invitation from Commander Sudcliffe personally. The invitation mentioned the day, the train, and the hour. Seeing the hour, Mr.

Ormsby paused to look at his own watch. With the folder in hand he walked to the stairs, opened the door a notch, and called: "Ohhh, Mother—"

No answer, naturally.

" 'My dear *Mrs.* Ormsby—' " he began, and read through, taking each word slowly, the official invitation of Commander Hugh Sudcliffe, USN.

No answer.

" 'My dear Mrs. Ormsby—' " he began again, but skipped ahead to the mention of the day, the train from Philly, and the hour they would arrive in New York. He followed this, quoting from memory, with the reply he had written for Mother, and the one she had signed, *Violet Ames Ormsby*, in her Aztec-brown ink.

When he finished he found himself gazing, through slightly moist eyes, at the picture of Mother leading the birdlore hike in the Poconos. This picture bore the title LOCAL WOMAN HEADS DAWN BUSTERS, and marked Mother's first appearance on the National birdlore scene. It was not one of her best pictures, as it dated from the early twenties and those hipless dresses, and round bucket hats, were not Mother's type. This picture had appeared—perhaps it was the only picture of Mother that the *Bulletin* had—on the front page of the paper when the news came through that the boy was a hero. Until they saw that picture, and the article with it, some people had forgotten that the boy was missing, and most of them seemed to think that it was pretty smart to swap him for a boat. "How's that boat of yours coming along, Ormsby?" they would say. No one had ever showed that much interest in the boy. Whose boy? Well, that was just the point. But everyone agreed that Ormsby was a fine name for a boat.

"Warren—" she said.

It came as such a surprise he just stood there. The draft blowing from her room was cool on his face.

"Ohhh Warren—" she repeated.

"Yes, Mother—" he said.

"However I might feel personally, I have *his* name to think of. I am not one of these people free to do as they like— Warren, are you listening?"

"Yes, Mother," he answered.

"—with their life." She closed the door, then opened it again and said: "You say it is blue for Navy?"

"For the Army it's brown, Mother," he said, "for the Navy it's blue."

MOTHER

*A*d astra per aspera, Mrs. Dinardo, and in the dim light at the back of the closet, her eyes closed, she pulled the new girdle on. From one of five dresses—*any woman with more than five dresses, Mrs. Cleev-Clodz, should have the dresses and the vote taken away from her*—she selected the navy blue sheer with pink lace yoke and kerchief, short bolero. From a bookcase beneath the stairs, the top shelf holding books, the remaining four shelves full of I. Miller shoes, she selected navy blue pumps with cuban heel and small bow. *Oh, we're all of the flesh, Mrs. Dinardo, but between men and shoes*

Mother

you can give me shoes—I. Miller's preferably. Backing from the closet, she hung the dress from the neck of the floor lamp, then used the yardstick to push the hatbox from under the bed. The hat— something had to be—was new. Navy straw with Shasta daisies, pink geraniums, and a navy blue veil with pink and white fuzzy dots. She held it out where the hat could be seen, front and side in the bureau mirror, without seeing—*certain things cannot be helped, but they can be avoided, Mrs. Dinardo*—to what the arm was attached. The hat on her head where it would not be lost, the slip tucked up to where it wouldn't stretch, she seated herself on Audubon's *Birds of America*. It had proved to be just about the right height. From the right-hand drawer of the sewing machine she removed a round stone with a flat sandy surface, and applied this surface to the calf of her left leg. Counting from one to twenty, her eyes closed, she rotated the stone, with a Spencerian movement, until the new hair— there had been a small crop—was honed down. It averaged one hundred forty strokes per leg. She also gave the rough spots on her knees a sanding, the callous on her right elbow, and the shiny surface where she was expecting a corn.

The corn—seeing the corn, she was reminded . . . of something—and closing her eyes she saw Mrs. Dinardo's wide flat feet. She liked to take off her shoes, pad around the house in her socks. "You've no idea how it helps with the dusting, Mrs. Ormsby," she said.

Using the yardstick, Mother reached one of the loops in the phone cord, slowly dragged the phone across the floor from the foot of her bed. Lifting the receiver she said: "Operator, would you get me Long Distance?" then she made herself comfy, as it was apt to be a long call.

MR. ORMSBY

Hearing her voice, he came to the door and said: "Coming, Mother—" before he heard her laugh, and realized she was on the phone. If Mother laughed, she was on the telephone. She never found anything funny anywhere else. He often wondered why that was, but it was not clear to him until the day that Mother *nearly* laughed out behind the garage. She had found one of his new socks in the compost pile. She had held up the sock, but she hadn't laughed because there was no real barrier between them, nothing between them but about thirty yards of weedy back yard. If she had found that sock on the phone she might have laughed to death. With nothing but the telephone there before her Mother could laugh and talk for hours, and there were times—when some bill was pending—that she sometimes did. But around the house she didn't need to telephone—she could write him notes.

As he stood there she stopped laughing and said: "A bag, Warren—you have packed a bag?"

"A bag—?" he repeated. "Oh yes, a bag."

"I have Mrs. Dinardo on the wire—" Mother said, "and she says she can certainly take care of me. You and Mr. Dinardo—" laughing again, Mother turned back to the phone and said: "I'm just telling Mr. Ormsby that he and Mr. Dinardo can shift for themselves!" Above Mother's laugh, like something suffocating, Mr. Ormsby could hear Mrs. Dinardo guffaw. "Now you run along—" Mother said, then she fell to laughing again, as of course Mrs. Dinardo, who was listening, thought *that* was for her.

Closing the door, Mr. Ormsby turned away.

Then he came back, opened it, and on tiptoe came up the stairway, as the bag, the overnight bag, was in the attic. As he crossed the bedroom he saw Mother, her bottom trim as a mermaid's in her new girdle, squatted on the new autographed edition of Audubon's *Birds*. Her new hat was on her head, the Shasta daisies rocking with her laughter, and the dotted-Swiss veil trembling before her tear-stained face. It was a standing joke that when Mother laughed, she cried.

Mr. Ormsby went by, a little curious as to what the girls were up to *now*, but he hadn't the time to stand around and find out. He entered the closet, saw that the light was on at the top of the stairs, and on his way up he stepped on a fig newton, Mother's favorite snack.

To get *into* the attic he had to wade through a barricade of suit-boxes, and carry the last half dozen or so to the top of the stairs. There at the top, right at the edge where he had been careful to leave them, were the cartons full of Grandmother Ames's effects. A black net shopping bag full of old pine cones and conch seashells. That meant it had been eight years, no, nine, since he had put his head into the attic—a good deal longer since he had got his foot into it. He pushed three of the cartons aside, and then lunged, with one hand out before him, toward the corner where he had left his bag. His right foot, the toes bent up, jammed into something shaped like a bucket, and as his weight shifted he heard a crunching, gnashing sound. This sound he knew—as a boy he had stepped from the porch into a bucket of eggs, and now he seemed to feel the soft gooey mess around his leg. He stood quiet, his foot in the bucket, until he had fought his way up from childhood to where he stood, one foot in the bucket, but a man. As a man it occured to him that it shouldn't be eggs. They were not listed as part of Grandmother's effects. But as he could not see his feet—the light and the window were both behind him—he broke a sworn promise to Mother and struck a match. Not for long—just enough to see that it was a bucket he stood in, and that he was ankle deep in Christmas snow. In one step he had crushed everything but the tree. In one blow he had reduced all the pretty Christmas trifles to dust, some of it like eggshells, some of it like tinted fragments of glass.

On the carton he found behind him, he sat down. Long ago he had given the boy a gun—and after that there had been no tree, no Yuletide season, no Christmas in the Santa Claus sense of the word. Mother had said—but never mind, in principle he agreed with Mother—but it had been a little hard on the boy. The tree had been the one thing that they *both* could do.

Hunting the tree, buying the tree, hanging all of the beautiful things on the tree, had been something that kept them together for nearly a month. For a week they would sit up late together, just to watch the candles burning, as otherwise Mother wouldn't permit them in the house. Somewhere at the store—his foot in the bucket seemed to help him remember—was an electric cord and bulb set he had never brought home. He had ordered it the same day he had ordered the gun. The gun had come first—but the lights were going to be a surprise, a great surprise, on the Christmas that never came.

No, it had never come, but perhaps he had always believed that it would, as the thought that it wouldn't, that from now on it *couldn't,* was new to him. He couldn't grasp it. How did one grasp something like that? Naturally, he knew the boy was dead—he knew that as well as the Navy knew it—but what did that have to do with something like this? Nothing. They were two different things. It was one thing to say that a boy was dead, but it was another thing entirely to say that some things, these things, would never happen to him. That was to be a good deal worse than dead. That was to miss the very reasons for being alive. Oh, it was one thing to be dead, but what was the word for describing what it was to have been not quite alive? Well, he knew. The words for that were *nipped in the bud.*

Mr. Ormsby

During a war one heard them everywhere. Nipped in the bud was the way one described, the way one grasped, that is, that the Christmas tinsel, the bright balls, and the lights, would never be hung. That Santa Claus, so to speak, would never come.

"Warren—" he heard Mother say, otherwise he might have sat there, his foot in the bucket, and bawled like a kid who had finally grasped the truth.

"Coming, Mother—" he said, but hearing her laugh, with the snort at the end, he realized she was still on the telephone. Holding the bucket down with his hands he slowly worked his foot loose, then took off his shoe and emptied the tinsel out of it. His shoe back on, he peered around in the twilight for his bag. He had bought it the spring they were married with both the honeymoon in mind and the fact that he had never had a real cowhide bag. One with a man's nickel-plated toilet set built into the side. As an overnight bag it was a little fancy, for longer trips it was a little small, so he hadn't really used it since that trip to Colorado Springs. Strangely enough, it was right where he had left it, but over the years, some twenty-three years, everything from Grandmother's house but Grandmother herself had been piled on top of it. He looked around for something else. Not at all fancy, but handy—Mother used it on her Pocono bird hikes—was a black fiber case Grandmother had passed on. He had used it on one or two trips himself. Mother would let him use it at night if he was going to some place like Chicago, and it just so happened he never went anywhere else. He took down the bag, opened it up, and looked at a wadded striped silk shirt—one he had been missing, as he wrote the laundry, for many years. It was not the kind they were wearing much any more. He used it to dust off the bag, then, wondering what else he might turn up, he ran his hand around the elastic webbing at the sides. A pack of Gem razor blades, and a letter—a letter from the boy. His father was in Chicago, so the boy had written to him. It was

Mr. Ormsby

dated June 12th, 1935, and written on his Camp Sheboygan stationery.

Dear Father:

Mother's cherries are all ripe and the first thing you know somebody picked the cherries off the black cherry tree. However they will soon find out that Mother's black cherries don't get ripe until about the middle of July. They also left a nice red and green basket so that I can pick cherries off the ripe one. My own idea is to let the neighbors come and pick their own.

Mrs. Dinardo's little Jessie has the chicken pox. As a Counsellor at Camp I will have Max Wilson, and I suppose you recognize him as a great football star.

Next year I am editor of the school newspaper, The Gossip. My staff so far is as follows—

Editor in Chief—Virgil Ormsby

Associate Editors—Robert Horton, Maurie Johnson

Business Manager—Jimmy Ward

Reporters (so far)—Janice Young, Julia Billings, Mabel Eiseley, Marge McCoy.

The business of the Editor in Chief is to assign every Monday the work which the reporters are supposed to report. That means that every Friday I have my hands full. In practical matters I find that Mother is not much help.

We have been having some fine weather, hot weather, rainy weather, and dry weather. Right now it is dry.

YR. SON

Virgil

Mr. Ormsby sat there, not thinking, gazing vacantly at the cobwebs where the morning sunlight, high in the gable, filtered through. Then he

74

put his hand back into the webbing, felt around. He found something hard, like a kernel of corn, and held it up to the light.

A tooth—the boy's first gold-filled wisdom tooth. It had been filled—he remembered the day—just below the gum line. All to no avail, as just a month or so later—but right there Mr. Ormsby stopped, the tooth clutched in his hand, and felt that he was going to be sick. A feeling of nausea, as if he had taken gas for the tooth himself, made him lean forward and put both hands to his face. What had come over him? The tooth. Nothing but the tooth.

In a museum where he had taken the boy to see a mammoth, a great hairy mammoth, they had also seen the grave of a man who had lived, it was said, thousands of years ago. In the man's skull, still in pretty good shape, were most of his teeth. But it turned out that was something that science had done —a scientist had put the teeth back in his head—as they had all been found like kernels of corn in a handful of dust. Something about it, even at the time, had troubled him.

75

But that was all right, that was all right to happen to a man without a name, without friends or relations, without a home in the suburbs and a pension he could look forward to. A man who had lived, somehow or other, without these things. A man who had no future, no education to speak of, no doctor or dentist that he could turn to, and hardly a thing, as men reckoned these matters, for his old age. Neither Florida nor the Poconos to look forward to. What the devil did it matter if this man's teeth fell out of his skull? Or if they should be found, like kernels of corn, in a handful of dust? Who was there to care, who was there to worry over something like that? That was all right, and a different thing entirely for a man like that, who never knew any better, to die as he did and then have some strangers dig him up. To be found by people who screwed his loose teeth back into his head.

All of that was all right, as there was nothing in common with a man like that and Virgil Ormsby, who was a hero, and who had most of his own teeth to boot. It was not possible that they would be found in a handful of dust. It was not possible that the boy's soft hair, with his father's right hand tangled in it, would ever be as brittle, as dry and lifeless, as the hair on a skull. That might happen to some man who had lived so long ago that few men knew it, but not to Virgil Ormsby, lying safe in his air-tight vault. That was the other man's fault for being born so long ago. It was the other man's fault for having died just when he did. But it would never happen to Virgil Ormsby, who had the good luck to die a hero, and who was now safe from the weather, the air, and all crawling things. Who was safe, you might even say, from time itself. Who had the good sense to be born at a time when his father could dress him in flannel sleepers, with mittens and feet, and a nightcap with flapping rabbit's ears. Who had the good luck to be blessed by God, to have won five Bibles bound in limp leather, and to be known as Violet Ames Ormsby's only son. Very little could happen, now or later, to a boy like that. True, it might have happened on Guadalcanal, where it was known strange things occurred, but it would never happen to a native of Bel Air. He would be, whenever they found him, just as he had been. He would have his mother's soft brown hair, his father's cleft chin. And except for the one in Mr. Ormsby's hand, he would have all of his teeth. There in his mouth, not like seed corn in a handful of chaff. That's how it would be, as that was how Mother wanted it.

"Oh, Warren!" mother called.

"Yes, Mother—" he answered.

"It is now eight twenty-seven."

"Coming, Mother—" he said, and put the letter he was still holding back into the bag. He closed it with a snap, pushed down the clips.

"I've called Charlie Munger," Mother said, Mr. Munger ran the local taxi, "and he'll be here in ten minutes. Warren, are you listening to me?"

"He'll be here in ten minutes," Mr. Ormsby said, and then spent three of them just standing there, the tooth in his hand, until Mother called him again.

MOTHER

R EADY and waiting, her gloves with her purse, her purse with the eggs, the eggs with her coat, Mother picked up the receiver and dialed the number on the pad. When the voice answered, she said: "Is this Miss Scallywag?" then waited, as there was nothing Mrs. Cleanth needed more than a good laugh. Not even Kagawa— "Evelyn dear, you have a pad handy? Yes, right from the horse's mouth. One—give power of attorney to your daughter and also duplicate key to strong box. Two—keep handy list of items exempt from income tax. Three —bone up about interest rules at bank, and inquire how to cut corners. There's more, dear, but that's enough to start. I'm going to name a boat, dear—I *have* told you but you wouldn't believe it—New York. No, I'm leaving right now. There's Warren calling for me now." She put her finger on the hook, held it there for a moment, then let it up and dialed again. "Martha—" she said, "this is Aunt Vye." Turning her head from the phone Mother read, while Martha talked, the inside page of last week's *Bulletin*. It was spread over the back of the Empire chaise. WEIGHT LIFTER LIVES ON CARROTS & PRUNES it said, and she went on to read that a Mr. Sweigle, who ran a gas station in Upper Darby, had not touched a mouthful of meat in thirty years. He was now fifty-four, and rode a bicycle to work and back. Leaning forward, with her free hand Mother circled this item with her red pencil, then said: "Martha dear—I must run name a boat. Yes— in a pitiful state of mind result of what she thought was something out of joint—*physically*. Eyes in serious condition, perhaps glaucoma, and going in for Red Cross, Blue Cross, and knitting. Memory also, with shooting pains in back of neck. Myself put her through eye and ear man, but no trouble there. Verified that cancer does not act up that way. But by mistake—left her in hall while I ran to do a little telephoning—she walked down hall into wrong X-ray room. Treated her for bursitis right off the reel. Thank heavens was only a three dollar charge as specialist dismisses bursitis as silly, says trouble due to California man who used word *psychosis* very loosely. Only treatment needed is new iron formula. Aspirin when she thinks the pain is bad. He claims pain entirely due to under-nourished sympathetic nervous system, registering complaint through impoverished gall bladder. Cure? My dear, we're right back where we started with the little liver pills." She paused, then called aloud: "Coming, Warren!"

"Yes, Mother?" he replied.

"There he is, my dear. Well, I've got to run and name this boat." As Warren came into the room, she hung up. He crossed the room to stand before her and she buttoned the lower button of his vest, and unbuttoned the bottom button of his coat.

"I guess we're all set, Mother—" he said, then he turned and looked through the window to where Charlie Munger, at the foot of the drive, was tooting his horn.

MR. ORMSBY

I<small>N THE</small> Casa Flores flower shop in the Broad
Street station—in the rush he had gone off without the wildflowers—Mr. Ormsby asked for lilies,
as the window was full of them. With a dozen tall
lilies—they were given to him in green wax paper,
like an oilsilk raincoat—he ran back down the hall
to the escalator. As he rose toward the platform he
saw, hovering in the smoky gloom of the train shed,
several dozen pigeons making a racket with their
wings. Some of them hovered, some of them
wheeled about one spot on the train platform, and
Mr. Ormsby didn't have to reach the platform to

know what it was. It would be Mother. Mother feeding the birds. As he stepped out on the platform he saw that quite a little crowd had gathered around her, as they did around an old man feeding birds in the park. They stood watching her fish for melon seeds, peanuts, or whatever, in her handbag. Feeding the birds—the way Mother went about it —both pleased and troubled Mr. Ormsby, as she might go in for it, so to speak, whenever she had a minute to spare. This might be in a train shed, at a public meeting, or at the window of some doctor's office, and it might surprise you where you might run into a hungry flock of birds. Let Mother just dip her hand in that bag, and rustle the crinkly peanut paper, and some kind of bird, foreign or domestic, would soon appear.

Mr. Ormsby had once fed the birds himself, but he had given it up when the pigeons became so friendly they were more or less menacing. He had had to give up a Sunday stroll in the local park. They simply swarmed all over him, and more than once he had the feeling that if he didn't fork up they would hold him for ransom—or worse. To tell the God's truth, without a handout he was afraid to enter the park, as they would follow him like so many puppies down the street. And everything he did to shoo them off just attracted more of them.

He had found it smart to keep a safe distance and just stand with the crowd, as there usually was one, watching Mother and the birds put on their act. It was one of those naturals, something that never had to be rehearsed. He was thinking of that when he noticed the boy, a young man in a uniform, in the Service, who didn't seem to be aware of Mother at all. He was seated on a black fiber bag, and wondering why the bag looked familiar, Mr. Ormsby realized, suddenly, that it was his own. He had left it with Mother, but she had turned away to feed the birds.

The boy was smoking a cigarette, and although he didn't look particularly tired, Mr. Ormsby was skeptical about disturbing him. For all he knew this boy had been through hell and water, literally, and what would he think of some old fuddy-duddy who complained about him sitting on his bag? What would he think—? But at this point Mr. Ormsby remembered the eggs, and in spite of what the boy might think he stepped forward and coughed.

Except for the fact that he wore a helmet—such as the Boy wore in his picture—Mr. Ormsby had not remarked anything unusual about him. He sat looking at a newspaper, and on the page open before him was the large photograph of a pin-up girl. Appropriate to a man of his age, Mr. Ormsby would not have remarked it if he had not noticed the caption, in very large type, beneath. This read: O.K. Joe? Not that Mr. Ormsby objected—boys will be boys—but the face that suddenly looked up at him was neither young nor old. It was long— something like a bird's—with large staring eyes and a slightly bluish cast about the nose. A dark skin, but very pale eyes—and Mr. Ormsby would have sworn that when the boy raised his head the eyes snapped at him. They snapped shut like those plants he had seen under water somewhere, snapping when your finger, or anything else, peeks inside. Like traps to catch something—and that, along with everything else in his face, made Mr. Ormsby just stand and stare at him. It was just impossible to tell whether this was a boy who had suddenly aged, or an old man who had been kept in amber since he was a boy.

"This your bag?" said the boy.

"Now don't you let me trouble you," said Mr. Ormsby. "If you're tired and worn out you just feel free to go right on sitting there."

"I'm not worn out," said the boy, and stood up.

"Worn out" had not been the right thing to say, but before Mr. Ormsby could replace it he was un-settled by the boy's wet stare. His pale eyes had stopped snapping, but there was something curious about how they didn't quite focus on him. They stared, but *each* eye at something, as if he were a double image and only came together in the back somewhere. "Well, well—" he said, and turned to see if there were someone standing behind him— but there was nothing but the crowd around Mother and her birds. "Well, well—" he echoed, and then in spite of himself he did a strange thing, he stepped back a pace as he sometimes did for the camera. He stepped back a pace as if he knew this would put him in focus, and that the boy would see—they would both see—where he stood.

In a long life Mr. Ormsby had been called many things—everything, in fact—but he now saw for the first time what he was. He was nothing more nor less than an impostor. Not just himself, personally, but all old men. To grow old was to be an impostor *naturally*. This was so clear, so terribly plain, that he felt nothing, did nothing, and, stranger to relate, he fully agreed with it. He agreed with the boy that he was old, that all old men are impostors, and that this judgment was quite impersonal. He took off his hat—he felt the need, the compulsion, to take off something, and looked at the band that read W. K. ORMSBY. "K for Kermit," he said, as if the boy were about to ask him, for people always did ask him that. The boy said nothing, however, and raising his own eyes Mr. Ormsby was amazed to see how short he was. He was standing, and yet Mr. Ormsby could see directly over his head as if he stood on some lower level, or in a hole. But his head was big—under the helmet he looked very much like a turtle and he peered out from under it the same way. A turtle or anything that lived under a rock.

"Young man—" Mr. Ormsby said, "young man, I wouldn't have said a word but just between you and me—" he peered around to see if the crowd still covered Mother "—just between you and me you were sitting on some eggs!" He meant this to sound jolly—as a matter of fact he felt a little jolly, he felt relieved of something, hard to say what it was. But even as he laughed it occurred to him what he had said. It was impossible to tell from the boy's face—which was not laughing—whether he had thought of the same thing or not. "Young man," said Mr. Ormsby, "I want to explain that I have a few chickens of my own and that these eggs are *not* what you might think." This was a lie, a total lie, as he didn't have a chicken on the place—but it was a lie to establish a greater truth. They were honestly laid and purchased eggs—not what you might think.

"My father—" said the boy, although he hardly seemed to be listening, "my father says the chicken is the way an egg gets another egg."

Mr. Ormsby found this a little startling. It was very much like Mother in that it was a sharp remark but a little hard to tell just where it fit in. As the boy kept a very solemn face he certainly didn't mean it funny, but if not, what then did he mean?

"Quite a little puzzle," Mr. Ormsby said, "Really quite a little puzzle, this egg-chicken business. There was a time I seriously thought it to be the egg, other times I've been just as sure it's the chicken."

"My father," said the boy, "says it's the egg."

"Well, well—" said Mr. Ormsby, and pulled hard at his nose to hear a boy talk about his father like that. Usually it was a boy's Mother—very likely his Mother was dead. "Your father raises chickens?" he said.

"Eggs—" said the boy, "the egg raises the chicken. My father raises the eggs."

Mr. Ormsby

"Well, well—" said Mr. Ormsby and took out his pipe, blew a long wet whistle through it. "It just so happens—" he said, "that when I was a boy I handled quite a few eggs myself. I guess my father was about the first man—really curious how *our* fathers—about the first man to really go in for chickens—eggs, that is, serious. When I was just a little shaver I had the job of keeping my eye on the incubators—job in those days, nothing electric, day and night fire hazard—and out of every batch I got the little fellows that didn't come off. Had quite a little brood of poor little devils I couldn't bring myself to kill, wingless, legless, eyeless little fellows I had to hand feed." All of this was certainly a strange thing to be telling a perfect stranger: stuff he hadn't thought of, even dreamed of, for more than forty years. Striking a match, Mr. Ormsby looked at the boy but he looked just the same, it certainly didn't faze him— "Your mentioning eggs sort of got me started—haven't thought a thing about it since I was a boy—but when I was a boy they tell me I was quite a shark." And so he had been—he let the match burn down and singe him thinking about it—funny how he had forgotten all about those eggs. "Reason my dad raised eggs—he had a great idea to sell day-old eggs to the dining cars, high-class hotels, places like that. Great idea while it lasted, but in those days you couldn't keep the chickens alive. Cholera ran right through five thousand of them in a few weeks. But while it lasted—I suppose you've candled now and then for your father?"

"My father," said the boy, "is an expert."

"Well, well—now I'll bet he is. Well now when you candle you pick up three or four eggs in each hand—problem when I was a boy was having such small hands—then you hold them, two at a time, up to a box with two egg size holes in it. Strong light inside of it. Then you give the eggs a twist, something like that, which sets the yolk a-spinning, and as it swims by you have a good chance to look at it. From that look you can tell to the week how old an egg is. A really good candler—before I stopped I could candle seven cases an hour and grade eggs from five to seven grades at the same time. That was with a boy's hands—even as it was, one of the big creameries wanted to hire me, just a kid, twelve years old. Made my dad raise my pay to ten cents a case. When I was a boy ten cents an hour was considered pretty good pay, but there wasn't an hour I didn't make forty to sixty cents. Quite a bit of talk around the town about it, remember hearing one old man say: 'Ormsby, why don't you retire and live off that boy of yours?' Just a kid too—little shaver—" Mr. Ormsby put out his hand to show what a little shaver he had been. Also to get his breath—he was all but out of it—and wonder what in the world had come over him. He had told this boy some things that even Mother didn't know, nobody knew, things he hadn't thought of again until now himself. "Young man—" he said, "I'm Mr. Ormsby, Warren Ormsby of Bel Air. Mother—Mrs. Ormsby is well known in this part of the state for her—"

"Lipido," said the boy. "Pfc Lipido."

"Glad to meet you," said Mr. Ormsby, although he thought him a little abrupt, probably a habit the

Army had given him. On the whole he seemed to be friendly, quiet boy, inward type— "Boy of our own—" began Mr. Ormsby, then stopped suddenly. Very likely a boy still in the service would just as soon not hear of a boy who used to be.

"My father," said Private Lipido, "can tell an egg just by looking, shaking, smelling."

Mr. Ormsby had never heard a boy carry on about his father like that. To hear him talk you would never know that it was a boy's Mother who —but getting back to the egg— "Certain things," he said, *certain* things can be determined in the manner which you describe. For general cooking I can tell an egg by shaking, turning it in the hand, but for first class trade—in order to tell a storage egg from a fresh one—for first class grading you need the light. Only the light will show you the amount of contraction—takes place during storage—and after some experience you can name, within a week, an egg's true age."

"My father—" began Mr. Lipido.

"I am confident," said Mr. Ormsby, "that your

father judges an egg just as I do, depending on the use he has for it. For high-class restaurants, hotels, dining-car service in the old days—for trade like that I am sure that he resorts to the light. Even on a farm you can't be too sure that an egg is—"

"You are a farm boy?" said Private Lipido.

"Well—" said Mr. Ormsby, "yes and no. Strictly speaking just a chicken-farm boy. Town of two, three hundred people is every bit as good as in the country, but I couldn't really say, as my father could, that I was a farm boy."

"My father," said Private Lipido, "is a farm boy."

"As far as that goes—" said Mr. Ormsby, "I guess I could say that my people have been farm folk from the beginning. On my father's side I guess my great grandfather broke some of the first land on the Western Reserve. . . ."

"A western man?" said Private Lipido.

"I suppose I am," said Mr. Ormsby, "though I never put my mind to work on it. If we go back far enough we're all pretty much eastern—Mayflower and that sort of thing—but I guess I'm western if you just go back to me. Nowadays Ohio doesn't seem very far west, but when I was a boy—well, as I say, my grandfather rode out there with a fellow named Bailey, Jonas Bailey—reason I mention him my father married one of his girls, my mother. Well, as I say, they rode out there in a covered wagon and began to farm where my great grandfather had staked out a claim. To give you some idea what kind of people they were—"

"You have arms like my father," said Private Lipido, "is it you wrestle?"

Now as a matter of fact— "Well—" said Mr. Ormsby, "funny thing your mentioning eggs and *then* wrestling. Truth is, I used to wrestle quite a bit. Never really cared much for boxing—could never bring myself to hit a boy when his guard was down—and if you don't hit him then, how hit him? No sir, I never figured that one out either. Seems to me I began to wrestle right after I had my first nosebleed, which was pretty young, so I had an early start. The truth is I've got—had, that is, a ribbon—picked it up at the Chautauqua, hundred sixty pound class; lean as a cat in those days but always had a good arm. Legs were always a little thin, boys used to call me Scissors Ormsby from the way I used to look in them wrestling tights. Matter of fact, it was quite an advantage, other boys would take a look at my legs and more or less forget to take the rest of me seriously. By the time they did it was generally too late. Only boy that topped me was a young man—think he was older and smarter than I was—who had eaten something beforehand that just made me sick. Don't know what it was, cheese or something, but all he had to do was blow in my face—and that's easy when you're wrestling —to finish me off. You can't wrestle for ten minutes without breathing now and then—Oh boy—!" he said, and out of the corner of his eye saw that Mother was still preoccupied. "Well now, where was I?"

"You were back on the farm."

"Well, I really wasn't—as I say, town of two, three hundred people—but both my father and

mother were born on one. Reason my father left
the farm was to take over and run a station—railroad station right on the main line. Boy of fourteen,
fifteen years—what do you think of that?"

"My father—" began Private Lipido.

"Now the way he managed that was just by fill-
ing out the application and sending it in signed with
his name. He'd picked up the telegraph business just
by sitting around the station and watching the local
operator now and then. Man used to let him take
over at lunch, or whenever he wanted an hour off,
so he had some idea what it was all about. Wasn't
till five months later the railroad sent a man out to
check up on him and discovered that their man
was just a kid, picked it up by himself. One thing it
did to him, however, was ruin his fine Spencerian
hand—always wrote a fine hand until he learned
the Morse code. Something about telegraphing
seems to have ruined it. Guess this was why he
taught me, before anything else, to write a nice
hand—and why, I guess, I really didn't like the egg
business. I took a job that didn't pay anything at all,

about twenty cents an hour, so I could sit at a desk and show my fine hand. Been doing just that for forty years. Yes sir, I wouldn't have believed it, but that's just what I've been doing, showing my fine hand now for forty years." He stopped. Was there really no end to what he would stand here on a platform, with Mother away, and holler at this boy? He stepped to the edge of the platform to spit—he seemed to have worked up a lot of saliva—as well as the juice from the wet heel of his pipe. He spit on the rails, then turned and said: "But to give you some idea what those people were like—"

But right at this point the New York train entered the shed. From the heart of the crowd surrounding Mother a swarm of pigeons rose into the air, and in a cloud of dust and feathers flapped out the rear end. Private Lipido had turned, was walking away, when Mr. Ormsby shouted at him. "Mother—Mother!" he said, then: "No—the bag! I'll get Mother—you get the bag!" and without waiting for a sign from Private Lipido he hurried away. Or rather, he turned and ran, just as he had done when he had been courting Mother and wanted to forget something that he would have to come back for. He forced his way through the crowd that poured toward him to where Mother sat on the bench, folding her napkin and placing it in her purse.

"And *where?*" she said, without raising her eyes, "have *you* been?"

"The lilies—" he said, remembering them, and was amazed to find that he still held them in his hand. "The train—" he said, and helped Mother to her feet. But before he could get her to take a step, to move one inch toward it, she stopped and said:

"Warren!—your bag!"

"A young man," he said, "a soldier."

"You let a stranger walk right off with your bag?"

"The train!" he repeated, and steered her into the car. They walked toward the front, through two crowded coaches, but in the third he found a seat —a single seat beside a snoring GI. Mother was determined not to take it—but when others entered the car, led by a woman, she seated herself without another word. With the lilies, Mr. Ormsby went in search of his bag. He walked clear to the front of the train twice—right by Private Lipido, who had to stand up the second time and call him back. Mr. Ormsby had walked right by him because Private Lipido had removed his helmet, not to mention how much different he looked in a seat. He looked as big as nearly anybody, if not bigger, now that he wasn't standing up. The only suggestion that he wasn't every bit as big as he looked was the slightly too-big look of his head. His hair grew forward and over the front of his face like a roof, and from the back Mr. Ormsby had thought him just a big kid.

"You find a seat for your mother?" he said.

"My mother—?" said Mr. Ormsby, but without much focus, as even Mr. Lipido's voice had changed. Not that he had talked very much, in fact he had not had much chance to, but it was not the voice he had used before. In dilemmas like this Mr. Ormsby had observed that Mother always placed her thumb and two forefingers ever so gently on her lidded eyes. He did the same—but opened his eyes when he thought of the bag. It was there, however, and still the same bag.

"Have a seat, Pop," said the boy, and Mr. Ormsby sat down.

Suburban Philadelphia was as good as anything —even a little better—to help a man settle his mind. The row upon row of identical houses with identical plots of grass, identical steps, identical roof peaks —identically false when you peered behind—all maddening at other times, was somehow reassuring now. Mr. Ormsby stared at it all with a pleasant fixity, as if seeing old and familiar things for the first time. Mr. Lipido looked at it also—he seemed very civilian without his helmet—and scratched and fidgeted like any normal young man. The scene on the platform, whatever it had been, was plainly the result of his upset morning—his forgetting the flowers, and the way the boy had looked in his helmet. It was now inverted in his lap where it served him as an ashtray, in spite of the fact that there were more pin-up girls lining the bowl. He seemed a perfectly normal boy—in that helmet he looked a bit under water—but without it he looked bright enough. He looked very much like a boy who just might call an old man "Pop," which was not what the boy in the helmet would have done. Not that he minded, as a matter of fact— "Getting back—" he said, "to what some of those people were like—they tell quite a little story about my grandmother." Mr. Ormsby paused here to see if Mr. Lipido was listening, as he seemed to be a little preoccupied with his hair.

"Your grandmother—?" said Mr. Lipido.

Taking a deep breath Mr. Ormsby said: "Well to give you some idea what she was like—" he paused long enough to stamp the wet heel out of his pipe, blow through it. He had tobacco, somewhere, but what he had to say wouldn't wait for him to find it. "Well—just before we were married Mother thought she'd better give the old folks a look at me, as there's no reason not trying to be open and friendly about it. Not that it really mattered, as

Man and Boy

Mother always had a mind of her own—but anyhow one day we drove over to Hagerstown. I had a little Willys Overland then, nice little car except for the clutch, but we got from here to there all right. When we got in town Mother remembered that Grandma was very partial to ice cream, like she was herself, so I stopped at a drugstore and picked up a quart. We figured it would be just a nice and easy way to get acquainted, sitting out on the porch eating ice cream and talking a bit. I got a quart of fresh strawberry, and as luck would have it Grandma was sitting out in her rocker when we drove up. She had her feet on the porch railing— she was just a little bit of woman and in a big rocker they didn't quite reach the floor. Using the rail was the only way she could push off. She was eighty-some at the time, and though she looked right at you through her glasses she really didn't see you any too well. They were flecked like old isinglass, wonder to me how she saw at all, and as a matter of fact I think she looked over them to really look at you. I don't know what Mother had said about me—if she had said anything—but it was pretty clear that Grandma had no idea who I was. I came walking up with the ice cream, which may have been the thing that threw her off and gave her the idea that I was an errand boy or something. Naturally, it made Mother pretty embarrassed, and the more she tried to explain—without saying too much, since we were only engaged—the more she said the worse it got. While she was still trying to clear up who I was I'd gone into the kitchen to look for some saucers and spoons for the ice cream. Well, I found the saucers, but though I looked high and low in that kitchen I couldn't find more than one spoon. There were some forks, but you can't eat ice cream with forks, so I came out with the one spoon and the saucers. I took Mother aside to ask if she knew where the spoons were, and she said that I certainly ought to be able to find some spoons. Naturally, I'd given Grandma the one I'd found, along with the saucers, and then I went back again to look for more spoons. Well, to make a long story short, I went through everything in that kitchen, every drawer, every shelf, but I didn't find a spoon. I found three sugarbowls full of pennies and a man's sock full of Confederate money. Grandmother had lived right in the middle of the Civil War but something like that was not a question I was going to bring up. I didn't know but what it had some value —but I put it right back where I'd found it until I could say a word to Mother. As I'd been looking for about twenty minutes, I figured the ice cream was pretty well melted, so I took some glasses out with me. Well, no man will ever believe it, but while I'd been gone that old lady had finished off a full quart of ice cream. Mother had been so astonished she could hardly believe her eyes, but Grandma had finished it off, right out of the carton. I really don't mind things like that—as I say I think there's something about the old people—but naturally Mother was just about embarrassed to death. To make her feel better, I said something about how my grandfather used to eat three rabbits a meal on the Western Reserve. When the old lady heard that she perked right up. 'Your folks is western people?' she said. 'Yes Ma'am,' I said. 'Your face is all right, boy,' she said, 'what's your name?' 'Ormsby,' I said. 'Ormsby—?' she said, 'well why didn't you say so?' Then she turned to Mother and said: 'You going to wed this boy?' Naturally, that just about finished off Mother, after the ice cream and no spoons, but I had the presence of mind to say something. 'If Violet will have me,' I said, which sounds a little strange now, but was just what Mother needed at the time. 'Have you—? Well, heavenly Peter,' she said, then she pushed back her chair, got out of it, and walked off the porch. She went around to the side of the house and lifted the lid to the cellar door, hooked it up, and went down the steps. We heard her kicking around down there, but before I knew whether to run and help her she was on her way out again. She was carrying a log, a good-sized log of hickory. I ran up to take it from her but the old lady wouldn't let me have it, she walked right by me and down the drive to the car. 'Open the door!' she said, and I ran ahead to open the door and she leaned in and dumped the log on the floor. As I stood there she said: 'Well now you take him along with you.' I didn't say anything and she said: 'One of the last things Fred did was cut the old tree down and saw it up.' That was all she said, except 'Good-bye' and to wave at us, but there was never any doubt in my mind what we carried away. I've never mentioned it to Mother—something like that makes her pretty upset—but I never doubted that I had the old man right there in the car. Not all of him, but a big enough piece to get the idea, and I've never lost it—I've got him home in the basement now. One thing I noticed about Mother—in all that time, twenty-five years, she's never pestered me to bring it up. We've been out of wood now and then but she's never mentioned that log."

"Hickory?" said the boy.

"Hickory," said Mr. Ormsby, and put the lilies in his lap to hold a match to his pipe. As a bit of stem juice drooled into his mouth he said: "Just to look at Mother you might not believe she had much of that stuff in her. But that's where you'd be wrong—that's where you'd be wrong," he repeated.

"Your mother—" said Mr. Lipido.

"Mother," said Mr. Ormsby, "is what I call my wife. Boy and I both call her Mother. As a matter of fact I would say that most of it—the hickory—came out in the boy."

Mr. Lipido looked a little bit puzzled. When he turned from the light his eyes snapped shut as they had on the platform, as if he had caught something this time, sure enough.

"Your boy—?" Mr. Lipido said.

"Mother—" said Mr. Ormsby, soberly, "has just lost her boy on Guadalcanal. Boy about your age—landed with the Marines." Mr. Lipido stared at him so strangely, his eyes pulsing open and shut, that Mr. Ormsby tipped his head to examine his tie. His new tie with the faint red stripe. As the boy continued to stare he said: "That's why it is we are going to town—Mother has been asked to christen, then to sponsor a boat named after him."

"Your boy?" repeated Mr. Lipido.

"Something of a hero," said Mr. Ormsby, but it sounded so strange, now that he had said it, that he felt the need to elaborate. "When he was just a little tyke he wanted a gun, some kind of a gun—and I got it for him. A thousand-shot b.b. gun named DAISY."

As Mr. Ormsby said this, Mr. Lipido picked up his helmet, ashes and all, and put it on his head. From beneath it, like a cornered turtle, he peered out. Everything that he had gained Mr. Ormsby could feel slipping away from him, but he controlled his panic, stared at the lilies.

"The truth is—" he said, as he had to say something, "that I always wanted a gun myself, so against my better judgment I got him one. I got it—" he said, "without consulting Mother. That was a mistake—for I guess all mothers feel the same about guns."

"Well, well—" said Mr. Lipido, which was an odd thing for *him* to say, and his voice was just a wee bit hoarse.

Mr. Ormsby

"Why yes—" said Mr. Ormsby, though he wasn't quite sure to what.

"And how is that?" said Private Lipido.

Hearing this Mr. Ormsby remembered that very likely the boy was an orphan, or a person without a mother to say the least. "Why they just feel different about it," he said. "Different than you and I would. And yet I'm sure that if we were mothers—"

"My father," said Private Lipido, "is *not* my mother!"

Mr. Ormsby closed his eyes. He tried to assume a pained expression but he was so sure that he just looked silly that he opened his eyes again. "I am not saying—" he said, "that your father is your mother. I am only suggesting that if you were a mother . . ."

"*Lipido* a mother?" said Private Lipido.

"If *we* were mothers," said Mr. Ormsby, broadening the implication, "I am confident that we would feel the same way." As he said this with some conviction, even his voice rising, Mr. Ormsby felt that he had settled *that*. Mr. Lipido was peering at him in a rather constrained manner, but Mr. Ormsby felt sure of his point. "Mother has never got over it," he said, "and if you were a mother that is how you would feel." If he had said *we* instead of *you*, Mr. Ormsby was sure that nothing would have happened, but at *you* Private Lipido suddenly got to his feet. He did not seem to get any higher, but like a beetle under his helmet he leaned forward to stare Mr. Ormsby in the eye.

"My father!" he shouted, in a voice that carried the length of the car—then he stopped as if to reconsider what his father was. "To be a Lipido," he said, "is to be a father, and if they were fathers they would feel like we do!"

As Mr. Lipido's message rolled back and forth in the car, Mr. Ormsby had neither the will, nor the voice, to say anything. He stared straight ahead, hoping that Private Lipido would at least lower his head before Mother set eyes on him. "My father—!" repeated Private Lipido, but his voice was very hoarse, and he really seemed to have nothing more to say.

Mr. Ormsby

"Sit down, boy," said Mr. Ormsby, and the boy sat down.

At this point Private Lipido sat quiet and looked out the window, his helmet a little low on his head. Now that he had it on again, Mr. Ormsby was at a loss to know just which Lipido he was. With it off he was Mr. Lipido, a perfectly normal boy—with it on he was Private Lipido and might do anything. It was the same with his eyes, one moment they were the color of water, and the next they were like dark buttons with bright little lights. When he said "Ha!" his eyes went from the one to the other, and sometimes without saying "Ha." Mr. Ormsby had seen his own eyes behave that way when he stood in the bathroom, in the dark, and suddenly turned on the lights. But he had never talked with a person whose eyes did that right in front of your face. Part of this was due to the helmet—although Mr. Ormsby had never seen the boy, Virgil, that is, in a helmet—he was sure, positive, that his eyes would act like that. Even without a helmet the boy's eyes never seemed to focus on some things, on his Mother for instance. He had trouble when she was standing right in front of him. It was so plain that he didn't seem to see Mother very clearly that she had taken him to an optometrist. Eyes like a cat, the man had said, but this didn't explain why he couldn't see people standing right in front of him. Mr. Ormsby had felt it himself—the feeling that he was obstructing something that would be clear enough if he stepped out of the way. Mr. Ormsby usually did, but Mother was more persistent and she would just stand there as if she was one of these alphabet cards. The boy would always look at her as if there was something blurred about her, and after four or five years the boy won. It was certainly one of the reasons that Mother took to talking to them from her room, from the top of the stairs, or behind the kitchen cabinet. Along with this was the way the boy—bright as he was in other matters—was sometimes baffled by the simplest things. Most of Mother's best sayings seemed to puzzle him. "Man is a social animal," she often said, as it was one of her favorite sayings, but the boy would just stand there as if trying to remember something. There was nothing to do but just hurry out of the room.

Mr. Ormsby felt like that now—on the other hand he didn't feel like that, he didn't know for sure what he felt. He was still undecided, when just as quiet as you please the boy up and took his helmet off. He placed it once more in his lap, upside down for an ashtray, and felt about in his pocket for cigarettes. There he was again, his other self, and as he tapped out two cigarettes he turned to Mr. Ormsby and said: "Cigarette, Pop?"

Mr. Ormsby was so relieved that he went right ahead and took one although he really didn't care for cigarettes. If he left them alone they smoked his eyes, if he took them out he burned his pants, his coat, or somebody's upholstery.

"Young man—" he said, "where did you say you were from?"

"Texas," said Mr. Lipido.

"Well—" said Mr. Ormsby, as he was genuinely

surprised. Although he had not been to Texas, he had time and again seen Gary Cooper, so he had a pretty good idea what Texas was like. It was not at all like Mr. Lipido. "Well, well—" he said, "and what part of Texas?"

"You've been there?" said Mr. Lipido.

"Well—no," said Mr. Ormsby.

"Then there's not much point in my talking about it," he said.

That was so much like the Boy that Mr. Ormsby had to stoop over, untie his shoe laces, then tie them up again.

"Ten, fifteen years ago," said Mr. Ormsby, "we were all set to drive out that way—make a little tour of the National parks, so on. Planned to go out the southern route so we would have gone right across your state—spend a week at the Grand Canyon, then come back through Yellowstone. The boy liked the out-of-doors so much I thought it would be just the thing to show him what this country's really like. Never had a chance to see it myself—guess I was no more than out of school when I met—" Mr. Ormsby paused, blew the blue smoke into the aisle, "no more than out of school when I met *her*. And once you meet up with the little woman—well that settles that!" He laughed aloud to think of it—it was one of those things a man always laughed at as there was nothing else to do. Mr. Lipido, however, seemed to have missed the point. "I can name you the route," said Mr. Ormsby. "From Paoli to Hagerstown—stay overnight there with the old lady I just mentioned, then on to Roanoke. From Roanoke to Mammoth Cave, then on to Knoxville, Memphis, Hot Springs, Amarillo, Santa Fe. . . ."

"You liked the Grand Canyon?" said Mr. Lipido.

"We planned—" said Mr. Ormsby, "to spend a week or two on the rim."

"The north rim?" said Mr. Lipido.

"Well—no," said Mr. Ormsby.

"The south?"

Staring straight ahead Mr. Ormsby said: "A little

earlier I was saying that this was a trip we had planned, but owing to circumstances out of our control we—"

"You mean to tell me," said the boy, "you planned this thing and didn't go?"

"Life—" said Mr. Ormsby, then gave it up and closed his eyes, placing his fingers delicately on the lids. For a moment it helped, but just as he had been before, he was troubled by the look he *felt* on his face. Not knowing what it was—*really* was—troubled him. Not that he knew with his eyes open— he couldn't see his own face—but only when his eyes were closed did it bother him. This led him to open his eyes and say, as Mother always said:

> *"The best laid plans*
> *of mice and men*
> *often go astray."*

Mr. Ormsby was quoting Mother—whoever Mother happened to be quoting—but he was struck by the fact that it didn't sound the same. As a matter of fact it sounded silly, silly and sing-songy, so that he was sure that he must be quoting her wrong. Starting over again, he said: "The best laid plans— go phooey!" and threw up his hands in precisely the manner that Mother disliked.

"If anybody's plans went phooey—" said the boy, but before he could finish the sentence Mr. Ormsby had raised his right hand. He placed his index finger across his lips, which were pursed for ssshhhhing, and from which a loud hissing sound, as from a radiator, issued. It was amazing, perfectly amazing, to see a full-grown man, a little more than full-grown, do something like that. Mr. Lipido was as surprised as any young man might be and seemed to forget what he had been about to say. Lowering his hand Mr. Ormsby said the single word: "Sacrifices—" then wondered what else he meant to say. "Sacrifices—" he repeated, and remembered that he had seen the word, in bright colors, on a poster somewhere. He stared into space—three seats down the aisle where a large fat man was hugging a small thin girl. There were three dark stains on the front of his light business suit, and the girl's stockings were torn at the knee. They both looked very happy and the fat man was asleep.

"That poor kid is holding that fat guy up," said Mr. Lipido. "They ought to change around, put him on the bottom."

Mr. Ormsby lidded his eyes, then slowly turned in his seat until he was facing the opposite direction. Then he opened them and looked far down the car to where Mother, her glove in the air, was waving at him to look away. When others in the car turned to see where he was looking, Mother closed her eyes and played dead.

"Why—" said Mr. Lipido, "don't you and your mother sit together?"

"Mother—" said Mr. Ormsby, controlling his voice, "is Mrs. Ormsby—my wife."

"You already told me that," said the boy.

Mr. Ormsby waited for him to continue, but that was where he stopped. It was such a strange thing to say—naturally, he had already told him—that Mr. Ormsby was sure it was still not quite clear. "I guess I called her Mother," he said, his eyes blinking, "even before the boy did. After all, I guess I knew about it first." He laughed a little too heartily at this but it was a real piece of daring—"I guess I knew about it first," he repeated, before he saw that he had said *more* than he had in mind. The remark meant nearly anything, any-thing— "A mother is a *Moth*-er," he countered. "Not just your mother, not mine. . . ."

"What did *he* call her?" said Mr. Lipido.

"He?"

"The boy,"

"Well—" said Mr. Ormsby, lidding his eyes, "the boy was a little slow to learn to talk—for some reason he was just a little stubborn about it. I don't remember him saying much more than 'da-da-da' and so on until he was quite a little man. Living off alone, the way we do, out in the country and so forth, he really didn't have much excuse to say anything. He learned how to whistle, talk to the birds, and he got along with his dogs all right, but out where we are—"

"What did he call *her?*" said Mr. Lipido.

121

"Well, by the time there was any real need for
him to call people something—when you live
around the house you can just talk, or say hey—
by the time he was ready to call us names he was
quite a boy. Now if there's anything Mother dis-
likes it's the kind of baby talk some people go in
for, especially with little folks. She just has no use
for it, and she early made it a point that there was
not going to be any Mama-mama business around.
If the boy wanted to call her, why then he could
call her Mother—just as I did, I'd always called her
that." Out of the corner of his eye Mr. Ormsby saw
the boy pick up his helmet and blow on the ashes in
the crown. A little hastily he said: "You can't ask
the boy to stop saying Mama if he's free to go on
saying Daddy, and I was the first one to see the
point of that. He was more in the habit of saying
Daddy, since it sounded more like Da-da, but when
she asked him to stop, he stopped. He was a strong-
willed boy in his way—in his own way just as
strong as Mother—as I said earlier, he's full of this
old hickory. If he made up his mind not to say

something I can tell you that he never said it—"

"So what did he call her?" said Mr. Lipido.

"Nothing—" said Mr. Ormsby, and turned to see the boy set the helmet low on his head. "I don't want you to think," said Mr. Ormsby, "that it was any real inconvenience—as a matter of fact it wasn't inconvenient at all. Although he was a soft-spoken boy he generally waited until he could see you, and there was never much doubt as to who he was talking to."

"Phooey!" said Private Lipido, "boy, did he go phooey!"

"Young man—" said Mr. Ormsby.

"Phooey on Mama, phooey on Papa, phooey on the war, phooey on the peace—phooey, phooey, phooey!" Private Lipido said. His voice was rising, and with it, above the back of the seat, his head. Mr. Ormsby's finger went to his lips but he could not hear his own hissing. "PHOOEY ON THE B.B.'S— PHOOEY ON THE GUNS—PHOOEY ON THE WORKS!" chanted Private Lipido. "BUT AS FOR YOUR MOTH—"

At this point Mr. Ormsby did an incredible

thing. Placing the lilies in the aisle for safekeeping, he placed his right hand on top of Private Lipido's helmet, raised to his feet, closed his eyes, and pushed. He knew, even as he pushed, that he owed this strange power to Mother who had once disciplined the boy with the same strategy. The sensation was that of ducking heads that had been bobbing for apples, and as the head went down Mr. Ormsby waited for bubbles to rise. There were no bubbles, but after a moment there was a noticeable blubbering, unmistakable, and the helmet did not bob up. Private Lipido was bawling, and with the same hand that had squelched him, Mr. Ormsby sat down and drew the helmet to his lap. "Easy-easy boy," he said, "easy, easy now—easy boy," which was what his father had said to horses, but which Mr. Ormsby, until this moment, had said to no one. He said nothing more but moved his hand to Private Lipido's shoulder, and the lilies to keep the light off of his face. They were crossing the Delaware River and he saw that it was dark with eroded topsoil, the cream of the land, just as Mother had said.

MOTHER

I N HER birdlore lectures, "Pecks at my Window," Mother sometimes referred to Texas as The Land of Wings, Mother Nature's Frontier, and other such terms. In reply to a question from the floor, Mother had admitted, publicly, that it had been in Texas that she first heard the call of the wild wings. It was in Texas that she knew the taste of wild meat. It all might have stayed in Texas except for Mother's gift, when publicly pressed, to put her answer in a few indelible words.

"He who knows the taste of wild meat—" Mother said "—or the whirr of wild migrating wings, will never in his inmost heart be content with domestic fare."

Thousands of Early Birds had wanted to know just where, on the map of Texas, a man could find this bird haven and wild meat cafeteria rolled into one. Others referred to the spot as the Texas Shangri-La. To them all Mother had replied:

"To all those who have so kindly queried as to my early life in Texas, I can only say that the thoughts of youth are long, long thoughts."

In her cryptic way, as usual, Mother was speaking the truth. The one long thought of her youth came to her whenever she thought of Texas, and anything unusual made her think of Texas, naturally. Anything good, or unusually bad, anything that took on enormous proportions (the Universe, Russia, the Hope Diamond) made her think of Texas, or Mother Nature, automatically. So did Trenton and the Jersey marshes nearing New York.

With her father, who had been a brakeman on the Pennsylvania Railroad, and rode on a pass, she had gone to Amarillo to visit her Uncle Dwight. In

Amarillo the streets were mud, red flares were burning in the railroad yards, and all night long the windows rattled in a strong wind. In the morning they rented a buggy and drove off toward her uncle's farm.

As Violet Ames had never seen the sea, or any large open body of water, she had no way to describe what her father called the Panhandle. The land seemed to roll like the wooden floors in amusement parks. Without seeming to rise, or to move, the land seemed to glide away from them, receding, and though the horse clopped on, the buggy itself never seemed to move. Here and there she saw great herds of white-faced cattle—Herefords, her father called them—standing in silent rows along endless fences, staring at her. They gave her the impression they had never seen a little girl before. They were always there, like faces painted on the sky, when she turned and looked.

And then they came, it seemed very suddenly, on the farm. When her father dropped the rail at the foot of the lane she had the feeling that the state of

Texas, along with everything in it, lay at the bottom of a sky-colored sea. That she and her father were some kind of crabs at the bottom of it. And her uncle's house looked like an ark, one that had long ago, at the beginning of the world, failed to survive the forty days of rain, and the forty nights. It had sunk, and this was its final resting place. Nothing seemed to belong where she saw it, everything had the look of having been lost, having fallen off a wagon, or forgotten when the owners fled at night. And there was nothing, nothing whatsoever, to bring them back. They had had reason to flee, and nothing they had left would bring them back.

It had all looked so unreal that her father had stopped—they just sat there in the buggy—when several small boys, like a pack of dogs, ran from behind the house. They each had a long splinter of glass, clasped like a dagger, and as they ran forward, hooting like Indians, she had put her face in her father's lap and closed her eyes. That was where she was when she heard a voice say:

"Skee-daddle you little bastards!" Then it added:

"One of these times, Roy, them little rascals is goin' to scalp someone."

"This is your Uncle Dwight," her father said, and when the man lifted her down from the buggy she saw the dirt, like decay, caked around the roots of his teeth. Dust that had banked there like earth around a pole. "Nellie could use a little girl like this—" he said, "instead of so many of these little bastards," and then he put her down right there on the level with one of them. She was nine years old at the time, but this was the first boy that she remembered, and his yellow hair, growing down around his head, seemed to grow out of his eyes. His teeth were large, and he brandished his glass dagger at her. She had never hurt or struck a living thing—not up until that moment—so it was strange how hard she really hit him, and how well she aimed. It made a dark red splotch, like the skin of an apple, on the side of his face. Nothing like that had ever happened before, and even before her father picked her up, she knew what she knew, and that it would stand by her for life. In dealing with

the male, use the element of surprise. All the time
she was there, several days more, that boy never
took his eyes off of her, nor did he ever again bran-
dish his knife, or anything else. Right off the bat he
was quite a bit the same as Warren had been.

They had walked from there into the house,
where she had eaten meat that had lead b.b.'s in it,
and she made a little pile of the shot at the side of
her plate. Only after she was through did she learn
it was duck. Wild duck, and they flew over the
house at night. The noise they made woke her up,
and when she sat up in bed she saw her Uncle
Dwight, standing there at the door, with only his
nightshirt on. Over his arm he held a double-
barreled shotgun. Outside somewhere she could
hear the boys hooting, and the morning sky she
could see through the door was suddenly dark, as
thousands of birds took to the air. The sky itself
seemed to swim, like minnows, past the open door.
And right then she knew—as if she had known forever—whose side she was on. She called aloud just
as her uncle, his foot in the door, shot off both bar-

rels, and that was all she remembered till her father came for her. He found her curled up under the covers at the foot of the bed. On the train she unbent a little, and not knowing that it, too, was a bird, she ate fried chicken for three nights in a row. It was looking up chickens that got her interested in other birds. It was looking up birds that got her interested in principles. Standing on principles she met Warren Ormsby, had one son, Virgil Ormsby, and lost him only to find him, as the passage said. Closing her eyes she saw before her a nameless boat. Opening her eyes she saw the river, and out over the river was a gull, *Larus atricilla*, laughing his long strident laugh.

MR. ORMSBY

O<small>VER</small> the river were the gulls, low and high flying, among them those that bred on the grassy salt marshes, and those that bred on the prairies and wintered, sensibly, in Florida. A lovely sight, and it soothed Mr. Ormsby's troubled mind. The head in his lap seemed to be asleep, every now and then snoring a little, and people in the car turned to look at them, happily. Father and son, one might say, the boy probably home from a stint at the front, his weary head at last at rest in his father's lap. So they seemed to think, and Mr. Ormsby let them. His own thoughts, like the wheeling gulls, were some place between the earth and high heaven, a place reserved for all those things that were *nipped in the bud*. For young men, taken in their youth, for lovers, taken in their blossom, and for old men in the sere and yellow leaf. Taken? No, they had never been touched. That was the hell of it. They were in the leaf without ever having been in the bud.

Now when he, Warren K. Ormsby, put out a shoot, or tried to put out a bud, or would put forth a branch as they said in the Scriptures, all he managed to do, somehow, was strike someone. When he put out his hand some stranger usually tripped over it. Take that time in New York—he was downtown somewhere, on his way uptown to meet Mother, when a man came up behind him and asked him for ten cents. Never mind why, but he had put out his hand—with a five-dollar bill in it— and pressed it into this man's dirty hand. It was one of those things that often happened to Mother, what she called a visitation, and why she was pre-pared, *always prepared*, to feed the birds. In this spirit he had given this man five dollars, without a string attached to it, but when he turned away this fellow kept following him. Like the pigeons, he tagged right along at his heels. After asking Mr. Ormsby for money, and getting fifty times what he had asked for, he refused to accept it, he began to holler at him in a loud hawking voice. When Mr. Ormsby tried to ignore him this fellow took some money of his own, money he had begged probably, and tried to make Mr. Ormsby accept some of it. He kept yelling that he was a man, and could give it, too. It got to the point where people in the street took him for a thief, or a rent collector, who had taken this poor devil's last red cent.

"I can give it, too," he kept screaming, "you think you're the only one who can give it, but I can give it, too—I can give it till it hurts!" And with that he had thrown all of his money right in the street, right there on the pavement, the five-dollar bill along with a clutter of pennies and coins. Then he had run off down the street wagging his head and bawling like a kid—not like a man, but like a child with his fists pressed to his face. It had been the most terrible thing Mr. Ormsby had ever seen, or heard of, and he had just enough presence of mind to get off the street. He went down some subway stairs and got on the first train. He rode that train until it stopped, sitting in the small booth for the motorman, then he got off the train and called Mother up. He said he had got mixed up in the station and took the wrong one. That had sounded so much just like him—as she had said over the phone—that it had made him feel better, almost normal again. She told him to get on a train and hurry right back. So he did, feeling like a boy who had lost his mother in a big department store, but who had been reassured that everything was all right. That he wouldn't be spanked, and that his mother had not lost *him*.

Later, he had wondered what it meant. Now he knew. Somehow, Mr. Ormsby couldn't seem to help anyone. When he put out his hand some poor sucker merely ran into it. When he put forth a shoot it was simply nipped in the bud. That was how it was, that was the truth, and yet he went on putting it out—he bought 1000-shot air guns and took up with the strangers on the train. He let them snooze in his lap and make a spectacle out of him. His hand still rested on the boy's shoulder, and perhaps he gave that shoulder a squeeze, as the boy popped up as if he had stuck him with a pin.

"Where we at, Pop?" he said, and leaned forward to press his nose flat on the window. As his helmet got in the way, he took it off. In the reflection Mr. Ormsby could see the salt loops under his eyes.

"Easy, boy—" he said, and patted his shoulder, "we got quite a little ride ahead of us yet."

"Where we at?" he repeated, his eyes snapping again, "I wanta know where we're at!"

"We're probably getting near Newark—" Mr. Ormsby said.

"This funeral near Newark?" the boy said.

Mr. Ormsby winced, then gravely said: "My boy, this occasion is not a funeral. I think I mentioned that my son is something of a hero, and

136

there is the custom of putting the name of such a person on a boat." He paused there, as that should have been enough, but Private Lipido seemed to be waiting. "What they do first—" said Mr. Ormsby, and held out one finger, put the other finger on it, "what they do first is build the boat, then present it to Mother—and then they ask Mother—"

"What will your mother do with a boat?" Private Lipido said.

"My boy—" said Mr. Ormsby, "for the last time—" then he thought better of it. He sniffed the lilies and said: "Getting back to the boat, there's a kind of ceremony, traditional, I suppose, that calls for giving the same boat back and forth, so to speak. Sounds a little silly, but probably traditional. Well, as I say, first she names it, and then they give the boat to her, then she comes back later and presents the boat to them."

"Hmmm—" Private Lipido said.

"I can give you some idea—" said Mr. Ormsby, and unbuttoned his coat to get at the correspondence. "When you take it step by step you can see how it works." He handed the boy the package of lilies, opened the letter case in his lap, and figured he might as well go back and start with the first. " 'Secretary of the Navy, Washington—' " he read, then began: " 'My dear Mrs. Ormsby—' "

"That your mother?" said the boy.

"Mrs. Ormsby is *my wife*," said Mr. Ormsby, and wet his lips, as they seemed a little dry, " 'My dear Mrs. Ormsby—' " he began again.

"I don't get it," said Private Lipido, and creased his eyes as if that would help him. Then he opened them and said: "Pop, what about you?"

"Me—?" said Mr. Ormsby, "what about me?"

"Ain't you his old man?" said Private Lipido.

"Why, yes—" said Mr. Ormsby.

"Then how come this dear *Mrs.* Ormsby stuff?"

Strange to say, Mr. Ormsby had never given it a thought. It took him several moments to grasp just what Private Lipido meant. Then with an air of calm he said: "My boy, I have had the feeling—much as I admire your affection for your father—that your mother may have died very young."

Mr. Ormsby

"Well I'll be damned," said Private Lipido, just like that.

Not knowing to just what this referred, Mr. Ormsby paused a moment, then continued: "For instance, there is Mother's Day—" he seemed to see it beckoning out the window, "and the universal feeling that all men have for their dearest, and their truest friend, their mother." It was difficult, Mr. Ormsby could see, to avoid the more familiar kind of remark—but this just proved what a common, accepted thing it was. "My boy—" he said, "if you just had a mother—" but he thought better of that, and said: "Would the United States Government, the Secretary of the Navy, the commander of the boat—" he held up the pack of letters, "write letters just to *her* if that wasn't the way everybody felt?"

Private Lipido looked so stunned that Mr. Ormsby felt he might have gone too far. That was the clincher. But perhaps he shouldn't have brought it out. "Mother—" he began—but he stopped when he noticed the boy's head was wagging.

"If my old man got a letter like that—" he said,

"—if my old man ever got a letter *like that*," but the very idea seemed to be more than he could grasp. His eyes rolled as if he had had a blow on the head. "If my old man ever got a letter like that"—as he leaned forward his voice was rising— "I can tell you the secretary of the whatsis, the commander of the whoozis, the namer of the—"

"Son—!" said Mr. Ormsby, but no more, that was all.

"I'm tellin' you—" said Private Lipido, "there'd have been a damsite less heroes if the boys had known the old man would get a deal like that!"

"Now *son*—" said Mr. Ormsby, but again that was all. He sniffed the lilies, his eyes softly lidded, and waited for the boy to go on.

"I don't know this kid of yours," said Private Lipido, "but if I had a nice old man like you this *Dear Mrs. Ormsby* would damn near make me sick!"

"I must ask you to remember—" Mr. Ormsby said, and returned to the lilies, fuddled and happy.

"Where does this come off?" said the boy. "I

have half a notion to go along and see that you get what's coming to you." The word Mother formed itself in Mr. Ormsby's mind, but somehow was unable to reach his lips. Closing his eyes, his mouth, he returned to the lilies. "Where does this come off?" repeated Mr. Lipido.

Mr. Ormsby had not really noticed. This was the kind of thing he left to Mother, one of the few, and besides he didn't want to disturb his delicious stupor. He let Mr. Lipido take the letter once more and read for himself just where the USS *Ormsby* might be found.

"Brooklyn Navy Yard," said Mr. Lipido. "How do I get over there?"

This stirred Mr. Ormsby to say, "Now son, you just forget about it. Now don't you worry your head—" he said, hopefully, "about me."

"And if I don't—" said Mr. Lipido, "just who the hell will?"

The word Mother once more tapped about in Mr. Ormsby's mind for an opening—but once more it failed and he sniffed the lilies. "I've got a few things to do first," said the boy, "then I'll hop a subway and come right over."

The word subway jarred Mr. Ormsby awake. "Subway—?" he said. "Why son, why not ride over with us?" Mr. Lipido looked at him. For a long moment Mr. Ormsby made an effort to look at himself, but the image, or rather the images, were blurred. "We have—" he said, "that is, we are entitled—" and he sat up to look for the proper letter. "Mother is entitled," he said, "to bring several guests."

"Not me," said Mr. Lipido. "As your guest O.K. —as your mother's, phooey!"

"Son—" said Mr. Ormsby, "I'll have to ask you to remember that Mother is Mrs. Ormsby—my wife."

"Then why don't you say so!" said Mr. Lipido. Mr. Ormsby closed his eyes and placed the tips of his fingers on his forehead. "Don't get me wrong, Pop," said the boy, "you can call her anything you want to—but what's her name, doesn't she have a name?"

Mr. Ormsby

If anyone had told Mr. Ormsby that he didn't know Mother's name—his wife's name, that is—he would have called the man a liar to his face. But now, for the life of him, he couldn't think of it. He had called her *dove* for a while—until it was time to call her Mother, and they were the only names he had ever used. She was known all over the state by a name that was two thirds her own—that much he knew, but he didn't know her two thirds of it. It was on the letter he held in his hand, on the dozen or so he had in his pocket, on his shirt tail—but he couldn't remember it. He kept his head in his hands —what else was there for him to do with it, a man who didn't know his Mother's, that is, his wife's, name.

"Here's Newark," said the boy, "we could get off here and take the subway. Maybe we could save some time that way."

"We're going to be met," said Mr. Ormsby, "by the captain at the station. If it's like the christening we'll all go over by car."

"I'd rather get over by myself," said the boy.

"I don't want your mother to be put out any—"

"Son—" said Mr. Ormsby, "I'll have to ask you to please keep in mind—"

"I don't want *her* to be put out a bit," said Mr. Lipido.

"Now Son—" said Mr. Ormsby, "you just leave Mother to me—leave her to me," he said, and three times wagged his head. And the boy left it to him as they crossed the flat marshes east of Newark, the tall grass blowing in the wind from the sea. As they entered the tunnel, and the lights came on, the full weight of what he had done settled on Mr. Ormsby like the pressure he felt in his ears. The idea that Mother would let him take a stranger, and a soldier at that, to this private ceremony was simply unthinkable. Mad, that was all it was, with her special aversion for soldiers—American soldiers especially. As the train started to climb and people stood up to reach for their bags, Mr. Ormsby's panic throbbed in his throat. But as he stood up he saw, at the end of the car, four or five more soldiers, two of them with their arms about each other's waists. A fine comradely sight, and Mr. Ormsby jumped at it.

"Son—" he said, and turned to look once more at Mr. Lipido, who was holding his helmet, preparing to put it on. Before this should happen Mr. Ormsby said: "I'll tell you what we'll do to make it easy for Mother, it's her day, and there's just no use upsetting her. She's got to stand up and make a speech, before a lot of people, and I'm here to tell you that that takes nerve."

Mr. Lipido put on his helmet, peered out from beneath.

"I'll tell you what you do," said Mr. Ormsby, knowing that his time was running out, "now I'll tell you just what to do. You just say—if anybody asks you—you just say you were a personal friend of the boy's, say you knew him before he got to Guadalcanal. Say you read about the boat, its being presented, so forth—and since you were a personal friend of the boy you—"

"Boy-boy-boy!" said Private Lipido. "Didn't your Mother give him a name?"

"Virgil," said Mr. Ormsby. "Virgil Ormsby—

you can say that you read about the ceremony, and if Mother asks you—"

"Mother-mother-mother-mother—" said Private Lipido, his eyes snapping, "boy-boy—BOY!"

At the end of his rope, Mr. Ormsby hurriedly reached for his bag. *Naturally*, he forgot about the eggs until he thought he heard something inside . . .

"If anybody asks *you*," said Private Lipido, "say you are a good friend of the boy. Say you are good old personal friend of the boy-boy—BOY!"

As the train braked, Mr. Ormsby said: "Now son, you keep an eye on the bag—I've got to run back here and take care of Mother."

"Mother-mother-mother-mother—" chanted Private Lipido, "mother-mother-mother-mother——boy-boy-boy-BOY!" As it was too late to squelch him, too late for anything, Mr. Ormsby turned with the lilies, forgetting his hat, and half ran toward Mother, who was waving her glove at him.

MOTHER

As he rose with the lilies from the chair, his free hand plying at his bottom, she saw that he would never, never in his life remember in time. When he sat too long—and merciful heaven ten minutes was long enough without his apron or his hat in his lap. Ten minutes was long enough to loosen every button on his pants, and without his hat, his overcoat, there was nothing but his shorts. She raised her hand, her glove, but as he turned and came striding toward her she saw—they all saw —a flash of blue polka dots. Oh Mrs. Dinardo, a law prohibiting seats facing the aisle, on the present level, outside of that nothing, *nothing* was any use. Her eyes closed she waited until he was there, panting, beside her, and then she spelled out, very slowly: "B-u-double t-o-n." He was gone immediately, toward the front of the car—then he was back so soon that she was afraid to look at him.

"Now what do you think," he said. "Mother, now what do you think?"

"I think it is about time—" she began, "that—"

"A young man—" he said, but she didn't hear the rest of it, as she always stopped listening whenever he interrupted her. "Golly Mother," he said, "I'm sorry, but—this young fellow, Mr. Lipido, turns out to be an old friend of the boy." If there was one thing she couldn't stand it was hearing him say "the boy," as if his son didn't have a name of his own. "Virgil," he said, "an old friend of Virgil's —and can you imagine me finding this boy on his way to hear you give the Navy the boat?"

"I didn't think *anybody* could come," she said.

"This young man was with Virgil in the Pacific!" His voice was so loud, so hoarse—she had never in

148

her life heard him hoarse from *talking*—she raised her hand to sssshhh at him. "Private Lipido," he said, just as loud, and in a way that was not at all like him, "—is not *anybody!*"

"All I'm saying," she said, "was that I thought this was a private, intimate affair, and I didn't suppose for a minute that the general public could come."

"This boy—" Warren said, in a voice so loud she had to put her hand on him, "this boy is not the *public!*"

"All right, all right," she said, but when she looked at his face she could hardly believe her eyes; his lip was trembling. She hadn't seen him upset like this by anything, not anything, since she called the pound to come for the boy's dogs. "If it's all right with the Navy," she said, "I suppose he's perfectly free to attend."

"When I see a boy on the road," he said, "a boy in the Service—I give him a ride. What would the boy—would Virgil—think if I just drove right by one of his old friends?"

"We're not driving right by," she said.

"That's just what I thought," he said. "As a matter of fact, that's just what I said."

There was more to this than met the eye—ear, that is—but she had to stand up to let the soldier on the inside out. And in the aisle there was nothing to do but get off the train. In Philadelphia she would go right downstairs and up the other side and go home on the local, but in a place like this she didn't know what to do.

As she stepped off the train a line was forming at the escalator and she hurried to join it; after all a line was a line. As she rose from the platform she could see that one of the cars was not unloading, and that someone—merciful heavens, it was Warren—was blocking it up. The belt on his coat had caught on something, and a soldier, a man in a helmet, was directing things. A regular traffic jam, and she could hear the soldier shouting: "Back, *back!*" and as they all backed he said: "Easy now —easy, easy boys!" It was certainly wonderful to

think what the Army had done for little boys like
that, some of them no larger than Boy Scouts
seemed to be. "Easy now—easy, easy boys!" he
said, and though he was the only boy in the line
all of the men did just what he told them to do.

"Lady—" said the man on the step below her,
"watch your step—here's where you get off."

She had just time to turn as the floor began to
slide beneath her— "Oh!" she said, but the man behind her gave her a shove.

"Just keep steppin', lady," he said, but when she
turned to say a word about *that*, the man was gone
—legs like Warren with that awful bend like folding chairs. Turning back she looked down the long
column of heads for him, up and down, twice,
but his bald head was not there. Across the aisle
was another escalator and she hurried over to take
it—let him look, let him look high and low for her
all night. She had the United States Navy, Commander Sudcliffe, and Mrs. Dinardo—she opened
her purse and looked for the slip with Mrs. Di-

nardo's address. She had it in her hand, when—
oops—her right heel caught on something. Then as
she turned the floor was skidding beneath her and
she had just time to throw up her arms. *And a good
thing, Mrs. Dinardo:* the left arm to Lieutenant
Pierotti and the right arm to Commander Sudcliffe, just as nice as you please. Not that she knew
till she saw the orchid—Commander Sudcliffe holding the orchid—*Pink when you name it, Mrs.
Dinardo, but white when you give the boat away.*

"Why Commander Sudcliffe—" she said, and
dipped her face to the flower, first closing her eyes
as there was often a wire of some kind. As there
was something between her nose and the smell she
opened her eyes and read:

FROM

THE USS *Ormsby*
Your Ship, and Your Crew
Commander Sudcliffe

"Oh, Commander Sudcliffe!" she said.

"At your service, Madame," said Commander

Sudcliffe, and would have bowed but there wasn't room.

"There is a Mr. Ormsby?" said Lieutenant Pierotti.

"I'm afraid so," Mother said.

"A blue suit—?" said Lieutenant Pierotti, and peered around, wanting to be helpful.

"The last I saw of him—" she said, and he certainly had it coming, "he was with a little man in a helmet, or a little boy."

"A soldier?" said the lieutenant.

"I am not prepared to believe," Mother said, "that such a small, immature boy—"

"In the Army—" began Commander Sudcliffe, but Mother's hand was placed on his arm.

"Oh, Commander Sudcliffe—"

"My dear Mrs. Ormsby."

"Commander Sudcliffe, I just remembered—"

"If there is anything, anything—" said Commander Sudcliffe.

"A very dear friend," Mother said, "five sons in the Service, four in the Navy, three five seven

East 116th street." Commander Sudcliffe swallowed, took off his hat and looked at the lining, put it on again.

"Just forty-seven minutes," said Lieutenant Pierotti, and nudged his cuff back from his wrist watch.

"My dear Mrs. Ormsby—" said Commander Sudcliffe.

"If a woman with four sons in the Service—" Mother said, "isn't worth forty minutes—"

"Perhaps if I—" volunteered the lieutenant, "waited here for Mr. Ormsby?"

But it was not necessary. There seemed to be a commotion on the moving stairs. As she was sure she knew what it was—a middle-aged old fool and a boy in a helmet—she did not turn her head, or do anything else that might flatter them. She stood her ground, her back to the stairs, and though she saw Commander Sudcliffe moving his lips the racket on the stairs was so bad that she couldn't hear what he said. It made her think of Lewis Stone, a favorite of hers on the silent screen. Commander

Sudcliffe was not *quite* as good-looking, but in the uniform—she lidded her eyes the better to see, to compare him with Lewis Stone. At this moment, the fiber bag struck her from behind. Not merely struck, but lifted—her heels were out of her shoes for a moment—and at this moment, as she rose in the air, she cried: "YeeeeeeeeeEEEEEE-IP!"

It happened to be, as Mr. Ormsby once said, characteristic of her. When startled, she found release through it. It also happened to be the sound, the sharp little cry, that the rabbits made when her father caught them in the disk plows. She had gone up, and when she came down Commander Sudcliffe was there beneath her, the orchid tangled in the gold braid on his uniform. Lieutenant Pierotti helped steady both of them. Her handbag swung from her wrist—swung gaping, naturally, with all of the peanuts and the bird food pretty well stirred up. She had just enough presence of mind to get it all covered up, while looking for some Kleenex— and enough good taste not to ask what had happened to her. She knew. She had known all her

born days. The only thing she didn't know was
how it looked—*that* somebody would have to tell
her—and there was just a chance—she let her right
hand slip behind. As it seemed all right she took
from her bag a roll of wintergreen mints.

On Commander Sudcliffe's arm, a mint in her
mouth, flanked side and rear by the Navy, they
went down the long arcade to where she could see
the wide street. Two cars and a station wagon were
parked at the curb. In the back seat of the limousine
sat a young woman, beige dress with red piping on
sleeves, boyish bob, starved young lady prisoner
type. *Miss* Sudcliffe—oh no, just as she suspected,
Mrs. Sudcliffe and *awn-saint* to boot. *Toujours gai*,
flat, hoarse, and tobacco breath.

"My dear Mrs. Ormsby," Commander Sudcliffe
said, "Mrs. Sudcliffe and I—"

"I have wanted to tell you—" said Mrs. Sudcliffe, pausing to pick the tobacco crumbs from her
lips, "how happy I am, *we* are, that your name is
Ormsby." As that was hardly Mother's opinion she
turned to reconsider Mrs. Sudcliffe. "Just imag-

ine—" Mrs. Sudcliffe said, "being a captain of a
boat named *Sinkquick, Rollover, Leadbottom,* or
something like that?" Mrs. Ormsby had not given
it much thought. Now that she did she was sure
the Navy would have better sense, better tact, that
is, than to make a hero out of something like that.
"If you're in the Navy," said Mrs. Sudcliffe, "you
just have to think about these things. And with a
boy—"

"You have—" said Mother, blinking, "a boy in
the Navy?"

"Not yet—" said Mrs. Sudcliffe, and paused to
blow a wave of smoke in Mother's face. Then she
patted her tummy, as if she held a puppy in her
lap. "No, not yet—" she said, "but any time now
—what do you think of the USS *Sudcliffe?*"

They were moving, they were even turning
right there in the middle of the avenue, and Mother
leaned forward to speak to Warren—then she saw
it wasn't him. No, he wasn't there at the wheel at
all, but in the car behind, in the station wagon. And
there beside him, right along with him, was that

boy. Both of them sitting high and looking bigger than they really were. As their own car swished ahead a small flock of pigeons rose from the street and were right there above her, wheeling, as they passed beneath.

"*Columba livia—*" Mother said, just as the smoke from Mrs. Sudcliffe obscured them, but her hand, which was already raised, waved to them. When she could see again the pigeons were gone, but a tall policeman near the safety zone, seeing her wave her orchid, took off his hat and waved in return.

MR. ORMSBY

I N GOD'S name who would ever have believed the boy would go marching through a station of people, thousands of people, crying: "Mother-mother-mother-mother-mother," as if he were selling something? Running with his head down, hawking: "Mother-mother," it was just a miracle that he managed to get as far as he did. He had had the presentiment—any man would—but penned in there on the escalator there was absolutely nothing that he could do. He could not reach him, it was useless to holler, and before he could do anything but close his eyes it was all over with. To the everlasting credit of Mother—where in the world would you find a woman that you could lift off her feet, like *that*, and except for yipping a little bit would not bat an eye? Who in the world but Mother would look in her purse for lifesavers and just as calm as you please pass them around?

Except for that yip—and that was a sound that she hadn't made for twenty-one, twenty-two years, when he had said "booooo" to her as she was rinsing out the garbage pail. It had been a hushed "booooo," he had meant it coy and not at all frightening, but Mother had straightened like a rod and thrown the garbage pail over her head. As she yipped the rinsing water had fallen like rain all around her, spotting her dress and making little pockmarks in the yard. He had not been able to move—what he had already done was so bad that he had not dared to breathe another word, or leave the porch and go to her. There they had stood, both of them, until Mr. Lily had come up the drive with the lawn-mower that he had just repaired. Without a word ever having been said—without a note to him or anything—from that time on he emptied the garbage and washed and rinsed out the garbage pail. For two or three years he had hoped, he had *prayed*, that she would sneak up and say "booooo" to him so that he could throw the darn pail over his own head. But she had never made a sound, never said "peek-aboo" or crept up behind him, never hid behind doors, or under the bedclothes, or anything. She had never done a single thing to get even with him. Except not to speak to them at all for two or three weeks, which was kind of frightening, but in a different way. In twenty years he had seen to it that nothing like that ever happened again— and it had been hard—for he liked to be prankish at the store. In twenty years—and then what did he do but pick up a stranger on the train who undid the whole business in one fell swoop. Funny how he had had a presentiment—but let God be his witness if he hadn't closed his eyes before he knew Mother was there. He had closed his eyes, but he had felt that tickly twitch in his ears that he got sucking lemons, before she had even yipped. But let the Lord strike him dead if there had been anything he might have done that he didn't do—except scream himself—and that might have been worse.

From his perch in the station wagon, Mr. Ormsby saw Mother raise her hand, and he leaned forward, as he always did, to see what she saw.

"What's up?" said Private Lipido.

"Pigeons—" said Mr. Ormsby, before he realized how witty he had been. Mr. Lipido laughed, but very gentle and not at all like him—or at least not like he had just been. "Columbus something," continued Mr. Ormsby, and seeing that Private Lipido was impressed: "Among the birdfolk," he said, "the menfolk, so to speak, wear the feathers. The female has more serious work to do." This strange statement Private Lipido gave such serious consideration that Mr. Ormsby felt a bit worried about him. If there was any comfort to be gained from what he had gone through so far, it was in the fact that Private Lipido had been impressed. There had been no doubt about it—when Mother had not even turned around, not once looked at him, the boy had been impressed. One might even say a bit stunned, for though it was Mother that had been struck, the full weight of the blow—as it always did—fell on someone else. Although he had never in all his life ever seen a woman in such a fix, even as it happened it was Private Lipido he felt sorry for. No matter what happened to Mother, what happened to you would be worse, and after twenty years he knew that, instinctively. His presentiment had been that the boy was up to something, but he had known, had *known*, that it wouldn't work. He had never seen anything that would carry Mother away, and the one sure way not to do it was to lift her off her feet.

"Mr. Ormsby," said Private Lipido, "you sure you know where we're going?" As this was the first time the boy had called him Mister—Mr. Ormsby knew that this was more of Mother's effect. "I've been to Brooklyn time and again," said Private Lipido, "but I'll be danged if I've ever been this way." The *danged* sounded so strange in Private Lipido's mouth that Mr. Ormsby simply stared at him. There he was, still in his helmet, but his eyes were not snapping and Mr. Ormsby looked squarely back at him.

"Son—" he said, "don't you worry but what Mother knows where we're going."

"I can believe it," said Private Lipido, but he said this with such conviction that Mr. Ormsby added:

"You bet!" It was a perfectly natural thing, when you got to know her you just *knew* it—so it was only natural that they both agreed on it. "You can bet your life!" he said, and then they leaned back together, their arms folded, and looked ahead where Mother rode. There was no mistaking the fact—even at this distance—that beside Mother this Mrs. Sudcliffe didn't look so good. Being the outdoor type Mother looked right at home in an open car, whereas Mrs. Sudcliffe simply looked washed out. "Don't you worry," he repeated, "but what Mother knows where we're going," and with that settled, his mind free of care, he looked at the park.

Mr. Ormsby

People were there, and he envied them. It was a very strange thing that a man who lived in the country should envy city people because they had a park. In the city itself he was crowded, in the country he was lonely, but in a city park he felt just right. The country was all of that weedy space beyond where the grass was clipped, and he didn't feel at all intimate with it. He had always agreed with whoever it was that said the most beautiful thing in the wilderness was a road. He had never mentioned that to the boy, as he had known right from the beginning that the boy would not find it true. If you're going to talk about two kinds of people—and you have to talk about them—there was no better question to ask them than that. Whether a man was a Democrat or a Republican, a Gentile or a Jew, was not nearly so important as what he thought about the wilderness and the road. The front yard was one thing, but it was how people liked their back yard that told you pretty much what kind of people they were. For the boy, life began where Mr. Ormsby was sure that it ended—

where the lawn stopped and the seeding grass shot up knee high. Mother had walked all the trails in the state but she had never left the back yard because there were no trails there to take. The boy came and went without breaking one. Only in the winter could you see how many times he left the yard, but in the summer the grass was back as soon as he passed.

"Mr. Ormsby—" said Private Lipido, "Mrs. Ormsby is waving."

Through the windshield Mr. Ormsby could see Mother turning and waving, pointing at something she saw in the park. A man—a man feeding the birds. His arm was extended, and a long string of birds, like a wreath of smoke, hovered over him. Mr. Ormsby stared for a moment, then placed his hand over his eyes wondering where he had seen the like before. Somewhere he had seen—

"My father," said Private Lipido, "my father is the one that likes to feed the birds."

Mr. Ormsby blinked a few times to hear this

talk of his father again—the same talk, but not the same voice. It was not so insistent, and it was amazing that his father, Mr. Lipido, should also like to feed birds. As a matter of fact he still might be feeding them himself if Mother didn't do that kind of thing so well.

"My father," said the boy, "fed them every Sunday morning. Instead of going to church he used to feed the birds."

"Well, well—" said Mr. Ormsby, and rubbed at his eyes, for the truth was that was how he once felt himself. Not that he cared so much for birds—not nearly so much as Mother—but there was something about feeding them. The truth of the matter was that the only time he had ever felt—well, religious—was when he used to feed the birds. That was a very strange thing and wouldn't make sense for anybody, but this thing that he had—with the birds—was religious sentiment. If there was none of this feeling in whatever he heard of religion, it was simply not religious, it was something else.

Man and Boy

"To look at him," said Private Lipido, "you'd certainly never think it, but the truth is that my father is a religious man."

Well now, well now—think of that. For the truth of the matter was that he had stopped going to church because there was simply nothing religious about it. He had learned this one day in the park watching an old woman feeding some sparrows, moistening the bread in her mouth before offering it to them. Up till then he had fed the birds himself, he had sat for hours watching others feed them, but he had never understood what it meant. But from her he learned that one fed the birds oneself. Watching her, he realized that it was a religious ceremony, this spittle she added was her flesh and the birds gave it wings. That way she rose with them, like magic, like everybody dreams of doing but only the old lady seemed to have learned how. In the light of this knowledge he spent one summer feeding the birds, all of the birds, and every Sunday there would be this Eucharist. It was an offering, a form of worship, that meant something. Sometimes he felt as if he had fed them everything, lock, stock, and barrel, and that he was like the empty bag he held in his hand. Other times the well-spittled bread seemed a message for someone. And so it had been, for as it turned out, Mother had had her eye on him and it was through that—

"Mrs. Ormsby is waving," Private Lipido said.

Mr. Ormsby bent low to see what it was they were passing. "The Metropolitan Art Museum," he said. For a moment it seemed as if he had heard Mother say this, over his shoulder, while pointing it out. As it happened he knew it well—he had once followed Mother to the point of exhaustion, then lost her somewhere in the American Wing.

"You sure—?" said Private Lipido. "You really sure you're not paying for this?"

"Son—" said Mr. Ormsby.

"Don't get me wrong," said Private Lipido. "I know she knows where we're going—but is she sure you're not paying the fare?"

"Son—" repeated Mr. Ormsby, but stopped when he saw that Mother was pointing out something again. They both leaned forward to see what it was —on the right, something on the right—and just then the car made a sharp turn. As they were sitting a little high, and on slippery leather seats, there was nothing their hands, or their pants, could hold on to. Mr. Ormsby skidded against the door, his face pressed to the window, and Private Lipido immediately followed to pin him down. Otherwise Mr. Ormsby would not have noticed how close they came to the light pole with the sign reading 116th Street. As Private Lipido pulled him back, Mr. Ormsby tried to remember where he had seen, or heard, about 116th Street. Somewhere, recently, he had seen this number on a piece of paper—one of those pieces that Mother left around the house for him. He put his hand into his pocket—and it was still there when he remembered that he had given that piece of paper to Mother herself. On it he, himself, had written:

Mrs. Myrtle Dinardo
357 East 116th St.

Mr. Ormsby

As he thought of this they passed beneath the Third
Avenue El, and immediately entered what Mr.
Ormsby considered the east side slums.

The street was swarming with so many kids that
the car slowed to a walk, and some of the braver
boys hung on the sides for a ride. Out the window
Mr. Ormsby could see tier on tier of fire-escape
landings, all of them occupied like boxes at the
theater. As a boy he had craved to know, and now
he knew for a certainty, what it was like to ride
the white horse in the center ring. Some of the people waved and leaned over the iron railings to see
better, and involuntarily Mr. Ormsby smiled. He
put on a smile, he waved and assumed a more public
bearing, although these were niceties that the roof
of the car concealed. As they came to a stop he
peered ahead—the windshield was the only remaining opening—to where Mother sat exposed to them
all. There she was, in such a bedlam as Mr. Ormsby
had never imagined, and with kids gawking at her
from both sides of the car. Commander Sudcliffe,
however, forced himself out, and as he moved to

make way for Mother he removed, as any gentleman would, his hat. Whether because of the commander's bald pate, his chivalry, or both, this in-
nocent gesture brought forth a cheer from one side
of the street. As Mother stepped out, gracefully,
the cheer gathered momentum and seemed to rise,
like balloons, from tier to tier.

It was a deafening roar by the time Commander
Sudcliffe extended his arm and Mother, with
queenly bearing, gave him her own. Mr. Ormsby
would have died, as sure as sin he would have died
rather than leave the car, leave anything, in a roar
like that. And where in the world would you find
a woman, a simple democratic woman, who was
not made stupid and giddy by something like this?
Where, but in Mother—and, holding his breath
as if the roar around him were water, Mr. Ormsby
stole a glance at the boy. Private Lipido's mouth
was open, as well it might be, as war or no war it
was clear he had seen nothing like this. There was
Mother, crossing the walk toward the steps that had
to be cleared of people, cheering people, who had

gathered to look at her. They backed inside as she came up, and there, there at the top, in all that bedlam, what did Mother do? Who in God's world but Mother would think of taking off her glove, waving it, and then from her bare hand blowing them all a kiss?

The applause was so long, and so deafening, that Mr. Ormsby and Private Lipido could do nothing but sit and listen to it. As the roar subsided dozens of people, full-grown people as well as kids, gathered around their car and pressed against the doors. Mr. Ormsby could feel it; the pressure was as real as if he stood right there among them and felt himself hugged from every side. They flattened their noses against the windows, made wet sucking sounds on the glass, and put in their hands for money, cigarettes, candy, gum, and to shake hands. When Mr. Ormsby dared to look he sometimes received a friendly smile, sometimes the razzberry, and sometimes the most frightful kind of face. One spread wide his mouth with his fingers, from which he thrust a wagging tongue, while with two other fingers he showed the red lining of his eyes. One varied this by showing his gums, which were stained black with something, while pushing his nose to where the nostrils were pits in his face. Others made the variety of sounds usually heard from other quarters, or stood as if dumb, their eyes staring, while picking their noses. Wherever he looked they were there, on every side they pushed, joggled, bounced the springs, worked the door handles, drew their fingernails down the glass, and with anything that would scratch they began to carve their names. Mr. Ormsby saw that they were an island, midstream in all of these people, and cut off on every side from the land. Now and then they were rocked from side to side as if crossing some strait in a storm, and then suddenly bounced, with a fine sense of teamwork, till they bumped their heads. The tires were thumped, the fenders twanged, new and different sounds were tapped out of the lights, the running boards, and the chesty hollows of the top. The thicknesses of the doors were determined, the sidewalls, and even the floor, beneath which a roving ghost periodically tapped. But through it all a small boy—his face did not quite reach the window—continued to eat whatever he had in a striped paper bag. These proved to be snails, which he held in the fingers of his left hand while with a hooked pin he fished for them with his right. Hooked, he drew the snail into the open and held it aloft to where it dropped, like a ripe grape, into his gaping mouth. As this took place on the curbing side, largely for the benefit of Private Lipido, it helped to explain the tight-lipped silence he maintained. In fact he looked a bit seasick—which Mr. Ormsby had felt was due to the rocking—but now he was not so sure. He felt a little queasy himself, and quite unconsciously began to practice a steadfast piece of Mother's advice. This was simply to refuse to acknowledge the disturbance, whatever it was, and had something to do with the word *cooey*. What *cooey* was he did not know, except that you did it day by day and obviously had something to do with birds.

How long they sat there Mr. Ormsby never knew. There was no telling—except by such foolishness as when it began and when it ended, which has nothing to do with how long a thing goes on. On the one hand it seemed forever, on the other he was never bored, or led to inquire of Private Lipido the time. Before he had once thought of the time, the mob turned their faces from the windows and looked toward the door where Mother had disappeared. As Mother was a bit short, five-one in her stockings, Mr. Ormsby did not see her leave, but he knew where she was by watching the woman following her. This person was half a head taller than anyone in the crowd, and her hat—which was drawn far down on her head like a bucket—crossed the space like a turtle on a choppy sea. Where a dip occurred in the crowd Mr. Ormsby saw her figure, strangely clothed, but undeniably Mrs. Dinardo. On her bosom rested Mother's white orchid, which reminded Mr. Ormsby of the lilies, the lilies that he still held in his hand. As they reached the car Mother's white glove fluttered like a bird over the crowd, and then the massive arms of Mrs. Dinardo thrust up, hands clasped. Mr. Ormsby had seen such a gesture in the newsreel pictures of prize-fighters at the moment they climbed through the ropes and entered the ring. As they would at a fight, the crowd roared, but above it Mr. Ormsby could hear the horn, or rather the siren, on Commander Sudcliffe's car. As the loud whine filled the air the street thinned to where they could move, very slowly, but nevertheless move ahead. Streamers of paper, bits of rag, paper cartons, and now and then a pillow fell toward the street, and until they reached the corner the clamor was at its height. As they turned, however, the air cleared, the street was as vacant as Sunday morning and suddenly as quiet, after such an infernal din. Mr. Ormsby felt himself conscious, but still stunned. In the car ahead the three ladies sat together in the rear seat, Commander Sudcliffe having moved himself to the front. Mrs. Dinardo had placed one of her huge arms across the back, her hand touching Mother, and her sleeve blew out like a sail in the wind. At the rear of the car, curled up in the tire, a small boy thumbed his nose precisely at the moment that Mr. Ormsby set eyes on him. It was not an impudent gesture, nor fresh, but one of such long and accepted practice that Mr. Ormsby recognized its finality. It was not at all personal, merely a fact, an oath taken so much in the round that it had a private existence and could shift for itself. At the first stoplight the boy dismounted, and as he idled by the station wagon he let his hand drag from fender to fender, the nails tapping. At the rear he joined with a boy who had been riding down with Mr. Ormsby, and then together, without a glance backward, they walked away.

MOTHER

C ONSIDER the lilies—" Mother said, and waved her hand to the gulls over the river, the terns diving, the gulls having better sense.

"Knock, knock, knock—" said Mrs. Dinardo, "knocking on the door she calls: Ohh Mrs. Dinardo—and a silent woman with hardly a word when you pass her door. One minute Mrs. Casey, I says, and runs to throw a sheet over Mr. Dinardo before I opens the door. Dead—she says. Mrs. Casey, I says, not another word until you have a hot cup of coffee inside you. Watch the red lights an the green lights I tells him, she says, and sprinkles

him with the holy water. Mrs. Casey, I says, now
what are you saying? You know how our bed is?
she says, and that I did for it was ours until the day
Mr. Dinardo sold it to her. Well I do, I says. You
have to lie, she says, so when you turn it is together,
and there was never a hitch in the matter till I pokes
him to turn this night. Then I turns myself, she says,
but there wasn't room lyin' back to back so I rolls
over and pokes him again. Twice again, she says,
then on her elbow about to shake him when something tells her to put her hand to his face. And so
she did, and there it was like a thing made of putty
and the marks left where she put her hand. No
breathing was there on her palm, nor sound when
she poked him, nothing but a feeling of putty
wherever she squeezed on him. Not a word more,
says I, until you have a hot tip of coffee, and while
she was at it I had a hot tip myself. Mrs. Casey, I
says, I'd offer you cream but this time of night, and
in the night air, it's better to have it a little black.
He'd die to think how he was, she says, a man like
a rock turned to putty—a Casey like putty, whoy!

she says, and I fills her cup. Mrs. Casey, I says, would you have me say a word to Mr. Dinardo, or do you think Father Murphy should be the first? Mrs. Dinardo, she says, God strike me dead if a Casey should blaspheme, but I don't think it matters any more. Mrs. Casey, I says, not another word till you have a second tip of coffee. Mrs. Dinardo, she says, God strike me dead if what lies up there is a Casey—no Casey was ever like putty, she says. Mrs. Casey, I says— Mr. Dinardo, she says, God knows what I've kept to myself from Father Murphy, and no good it did me as you can see for yourself. Mrs. Casey, I says, not another word— Mrs. Dinardo, she says, I seen him turnin', God strike me dead if he wasn't turnin'—but I didn't know it was into putty, she says."

"We are what we eat," said Mother. "Experiments with mice have shown—"

"When it comes—" said Mrs. Dinardo, "it comes. Mind the red lights and the green lights, I tells him and blesses him with the holy water. I kisses him —but when it comes, it comes."

"Mice fed on roast beef," Mother said, "have shown a marked aggressive manner. In other words, imperialist. On the other hand rice—beriberi— have kept the poor Chinese—"

"If it's dying," said Mrs. Dinardo, "I bears it with a little organ music—if it's living I would as soon hear a good man talk. Mrs. Casey, I says, the Lord made the Protestants to take care of the living, and the Catholics to take care of the dead. I would rather live forever, she says, and God knows I'm tired enough of it, than have to go to a Protestant funeral. That's just what I'm sayin', I says, the Protestants makes it easier for the living and the Catholics makes it easier for the dead. It's this getting up for Mass, I says, that nearly kills so many people. Mrs. Dinardo, she says, with all respects to the likes of yourself, it's the Catholics that take care of a man the best. We're here and we're gone, she says, Mrs. Dinardo—but we're not here long and we're gone forever. It's dead that you are for the longest time, she says."

Over their head was the great span of the Triborough Bridge, with the traffic crossing it like ants. Raising her glove, as if at a signal, Mother waved.

"It may sound bromidic," said Mother, "but Mrs. Dinardo, success is getting what you want. Happiness is wanting what you get."

"Well now," said Mrs. Dinardo, "so it is. Since this war breaks out I've had my fill of the finest shirts and ladies' fancies, all I can do—but am I happy? I am not. Now and then I throws into the tub one of Mr. Dinardo's drawers just for the pleasure I gets out of washin' a dirty thing."

"Excuse me," said Mrs. Sudcliffe, "but I just couldn't help hearing—"

"Yes ma'am?" said Mrs. Dinardo.

"I'm in a perfectly ghastly fix, just ghastly—" said Mrs. Sudcliffe, "trying to do Arthur's laundry in our hotel room. It's just impossible to do a man's things in a small bowl, let alone the pieces I have to wash and rinse for myself."

"Ma'am—" said Mrs. Dinardo, "I was just now saying to Mrs. Ormsby that I'm changing back from ladies to gentlemen's things. When I did just the straight wash there was only the clean soap smell in the house and never a word from Mr. Dinardo or down the hall. It's one thing for a fine smell to be stoppered up in a bottle, and another to have it loose around the house. A ten-hour day Mr. Dinardo puts in on the side of a boat, but not to come home to such a smell in the house."

"I am five months pregnant," said Mrs. Sudcliffe, "and the—"

"A baby?" said Mrs. Dinardo. Mrs. Sudcliffe nodded. "Ma'am—" said Mrs. Dinardo, "if you don't mind a lady who's raised seven boys giving a bit of advice, for a baby you don't eat enough."

Leaning forward, between them, Mother said: "Luncheon—we're having luncheon on the *Ormsby*."

"Sergeant Michael Dinardo—" Mrs. Dinardo raised her hand to a position over her head, then tipped her head, sidewise, to look up at it. "My baby—in the street he stops me and by his side I have the inferior complex." Shaking her head, her eyes moist: "All the same," said Mrs. Dinardo, "no name for a boat is Dinardo. If it is something that wants to be named, the Dinardos name the streets—streets are all right," said Mrs. Dinardo, "boats sink!"

"Mrs. Dinardo—" said Mother.

"In that case," said Mrs. Sudcliffe, lighting another cigarette, "they just give the name to another one."

"A street is a street, a boat sinks!" said Mrs. Dinardo.

"In a war like this streets can be blown up as well as boats," said Mrs. Sudcliffe. "And when they are they get a *new* name."

"If you live on Dinardo, you live on Dinardo," said Mrs. Dinardo. "Three five seven East Dinardo."

"If my husband," said Mrs. Sudcliffe, "should just stop by with some things of his own—"

"I'm just saying," said Mrs. Dinardo, "that Dinardo's as fine a name for a street as Ormsby is a grand name for a boat."

"I don't mean to infer—" said Mrs. Sudcliffe.

"Dinardo Avenue," said Mrs. Dinardo. "Broadway and Dinardo."

"Mrs. Sudcliffe," said Mother, "it seems to me that the name Dinardo is better than most of the names we—"

"I'm not so much as suggesting," said Mrs. Sudcliffe, "that—"

"And Ormsby," said Mrs. Dinardo. "If it's boats that have to be named now what is a finer name than Ormsby?"

"I was *speaking* of boats," said Mrs. Sudcliffe. "What people would like to call streets is simply none of my business, but as a woman in the Navy I—"

"What is it a street does but go somewhere?" said Mrs. Dinardo. "Like a boat—what is it it does but go and come? What is it a boat does a street can't do?"

Mother

"Mrs. Dinardo," said Mrs. Sudcliffe, "if I had a son in the Navy I would make it a point to know the difference between a street and a boat."

"Mrs. Cliffsides," said Mrs. Dinardo, "if it's the difference you are wanting, a street is a street going somewhere, a boat sinks!"

"My dear Mrs. Dinardo—" said Mrs. Sudcliffe, but she was interrupted by Mother, who was leaning forward, her arm raised in the air. She was pointing overhead at the dark hulk of the Brooklyn Bridge. A very marvelous thing it was, seen from below and against the sky, like a great bow drawn taut and about to release something.

"A bridge—" said Mother, "a boat is a bridge to span the oceans and a street is a bridge to span the land." Mrs. Dinardo pushed her hat back the better to look at her—Mrs. Sudcliffe stared vacantly toward the sea. "In our time," said Mother, "everything in the world must be spanned, everything is a bridge, we are bridges too. I am a bridge—" she said, and gave her left hand to Mrs. Sudcliffe, and her right to Mrs. Dinardo, who stared at her.

"A bridge too," said Mrs. Dinardo, "Dinardo— a good name for a bridge."

"All men are brothers," said Mother, and held tight to the ladies' hands as they left the parkway and rose toward the sky-road, the Brooklyn Bridge.

MR. ORMSBY

From the bridge Mr. Ormsby could see the harbor, the Statue of Liberty, and below on the river a small, narrow boat, outward bound. From such a height it resembled a submarine on the surface, or a large toy battleship put out for growing boys. Mr. Ormsby did not know its type—not very well, that is—as he had been absorbed with the problem of Mother and the bottle, alone on the scaffold in the christening ceremony. Very likely this was not *the boat*, but he had seen such a boat before, and this was why he leaned forward and pressed Private Lipido against the window.

"There—!" he said, "there he goes!"

Private Lipido lowered the window and peered out. As Private Lipido stared it occurred to Mr. Ormsby that he had been talking like the Boy, that he had been saying considerably more than he said. For boats one usually said *she—there she goes* would have been perfectly normal, but there *he* goes did have an odd ring. Yet Private Lipido seemed to have understood. He continued to peer below until the roofs shut off the view of the river and there was a sudden smell of coffee in the air. Whether it was this, or something attentive in the face of Private Lipido, Mr. Ormsby said: "No, son —his plans didn't go phooey." He said this with such conviction that it startled both of them, and they turned to look for the boat again. "*The* Boy and *the Ormsby*," he continued, which certainly meant nothing whatsoever, or considerably more than anything he had ever said. "There goes the Ormsby," men would say, just as he had always looked and said to himself: "There goes the Boy." *The* Boy and *the Ormsby*—it was a very strange thing that they both had the definite article. There was something impersonal and permanent about both of them, and this was why it had never worked to call him Son. *The* son, perhaps, but not just Son, or Virgil, or Ormsby, or anything like that. There goes the *Ormsby*, men would say, without ever knowing, as he knew, how absolutely right it was. Without ever knowing that this was proof that his plans went right.

Other men had lost boys—but until he met a man who had *found* one, he could hardly talk about this thing. Even Private Lipido was not quite ready for that. And then it would depend on whether the man thought of his son as the Boy, or as something that belonged to him. This was the real difference: he didn't—he had always had the feeling men must have who know that they had adopted something. When he read in the papers—and once he thought of it the papers seemed to be just full of it—about men and women who wondered if they had their own babies, he felt a very special sympathy for them. Not that he didn't love the boy—but whatever fathers were supposed to feel was quite different from what he really felt. Not that he didn't feel the loss—but what he felt was an absence that he couldn't seem to put his finger on. Some people seemed to feel a loss like that like some kind of an amputation, they bled from it, and from a wound like that some of them died. But what he felt was that he had actually freed something. What he felt was something like the difference between the fun in having slaves and the pleasure you get from liberating them.

"There she goes!" said Private Lipido, but when Mr. Ormsby sat up to stare he saw it was Mother —Mother waving for them again. Mrs. Dinardo's sleeve still blew out like a sail, but with her free hand she was now holding down her hat. Mrs. Sudcliffe had slipped to where she was all but out of sight.

When he was a boy—no, a young man—there had been a person named Floyd Collins who had got caught in the shaft of a mine when it caved in. The whole country had got concerned about him.

Mr. Ormsby

Not that Floyd Collins was so much—that is, no more than anybody—but there was a man, *the man*, people could do something about. There was a man who wasn't going to sell you a bill of goods, or cheat you, or make a plain damn fool out of you for wanting to help someone. All over the world there were people who needed as much help as Floyd Collins, maybe more, but there were always strings attached. You could never be sure you were really helping them or not. But the thing about Floyd Collins was that he was one man, in a hell of a fix, who needed everybody's help to get him out. The moment that cave fell in on him he was something more than Floyd Collins, more than any single man ever was or ever could be. He was every man who was caught in a trap and needed help. Mr. Ormsby had sent right off ten dollars—a lot of money for a boy at that time—to help buy coffee and doughnuts for the men who were digging for him. And the truth was he didn't know whether they had saved Floyd Collins or not. The important thing seemed to be to help him, to do everything

you could to save him, and if you did that, something bigger than Mr. Collins survived. His name
survived—which was more important—as it had
little to do with the man who was lost and a lot to
do with the man they had tried to save. And this
was how he felt about the boy. He had been born
into a fix at the start because of how he was, the
way Mother was, and the way the world happened
to be. It was a fix nobody seemed to help—anyhow,
not the people in it—like the fix that Floyd Collins
was in in that mine. Floyd Collins crawled into a
mine and the boy went off to a war before the real
fix they were in meant anything. The fix had been
there all the time—he didn't know Floyd Collins,
but only a fix of some kind would have a man
crawling around in a hole. And then hundreds of
men, maybe thousands, had done their level best to
save Floyd Collins in order to save what was all but
lost of themselves. Hundreds of men had risked
their lives. To save the Boy ten men had been
wounded, one man lost his leg and nearly died, not
because he was Virgil, but because he meant some-

thing. And every man who tried to save him meant something. So the name meant something: the USS *Ormsby* was quite another thing than the boy he had given a b.b. gun. "There goes the Ormsby," men would say, and maybe some of them would come to know that in this world his plans didn't go phooey, but went right.

"She's waving!" said Private Lipido, and Mr. Ormsby waved back before he noticed that Private Lipido had also waved. Then they turned, for Mother was pointing at what she saw behind them, which proved to be a stunning view of New York. The same view, Mr. Ormsby remembered, that Mother had on her telephone pad, and the lights of the city lit up when she left the receiver down.

Private Lipido was the first to turn and signal to Mother that they had seen it, and just in time, as when Mr. Ormsby turned Mother was gone. He did not see her again until they came out on the street that led to the dock, and there she was, pointing again, ahead toward the pier. And there at the end of the street was the *Ormsby*, looking more like a miniature than ever, but with more men lined up on the deck than Mr. Ormsby could believe really lived inside. She was drawn into the pier broadside, the full crew standing at attention, and on the dock were perhaps a hundred folding chairs. Some of them were occupied, but a large group of people had gathered about Commander Sudcliffe's car, from which Mrs. Dinardo was preparing to dismount. As Mr. Ormsby had not seen her enter, nor at any time in the round, he had no idea how large a woman she had become. The car tipped ominously, then rocked back to normal as she placed both of her large feet on the pier. A full head taller than Commander Sudcliffe, she permitted him to support her elbow until he turned away to assist Mother. Mr. Ormsby saw none of this, as it took place behind Mrs. Dinardo, who stood a bit straddled while she flexed her arms. Although she was an enormous woman, it was not entirely her size that made it impossible for Mr. Ormsby to see anything else. Much of it had to do with the dress—parts of which Mr. Ormsby had seen, and pur-

chased, during the fall of 1923. That fall, from
Chicago, he had brought Mother a spangled sequin
dress he had bought from a man in the lobby of the
Morrison Hotel. This man just happened to have
two very exclusive garments, just three weeks out
of Paris, and he was willing to sacrifice one of them
to a man with some taste. They were the only
things of their kind, and he had sacrificed one to
Mr. Ormsby, and the other he had taken home to
his wife. The part of *that* dress Mr. Ormsby remembered now extended to Mrs. Dinardo's waist,
where another dress, which he remembered only
vaguely, carried on to her knees. There both dresses
stopped, and more than anything else Mr. Ormsby
could think of, Mrs. Dinardo resembled an armored
Amazon. In the morning sun the spangled sequins
glittered like a coat of mail, and her hat was like a
helmet pulled down on her head. Even as he stared
she supplied the shield, the only piece of armor she
was lacking, by thrusting before her, and opening,
a red and green parasol. That she raised it over her
head led Mr. Ormsby to look at the sky, but for ar-

rows rather than for sun or rain. As Mother stepped
into the sun beside her Mrs. Dinardo moved the
parasol to the left, so that its shadow kept Mother
in the shade. Mrs. Sudcliffe was left to shift for herself, which she was still doing when Mr. Ormsby
and Private Lipido stepped out on the pier.

The USS *Ormsby*, a destroyer escort, had been
drawn in broadside so that the proceedings on the
deck could be witnessed from the pier. She was—or
he was—Mr. Ormsby remembered, just a slip of a
boat, but very tough-looking with so much armor
and the fresh camouflage. The crew—a large as-
sortment of rather big men for such a little boat—
stood in ranks at the back of the deck, waiting for
the ceremony. A flag was flying, and Mr. Ormsby
straightened a bit, as he always did when in the
presence of a blowing flag. Here in the sun, with
the boat, the flag, and a narrow glimpse of white-
capped water, Mr. Ormsby had the feeling there
was martial music in the air. It was a little festive,
and seeing that Private Lipido was a bit more erect,

more military, Mr. Ormsby controlled his impulse
to sit down. His first impulse always was—whenever with Mother—to take a seat in the back and
listen quietly. He really didn't like to be in the spotlight, or anywhere someone might recognize him
and say: "Why here's Mr. Ormsby, Mrs. Ormsby's
husband." He preferred to sit down—but with
Private Lipido so erect and military, he felt obliged
to join a little more into things. There was quite a
discussion around the car—or rather around Mrs.
Dinardo, whose umbrella dominated the scene.
With Private Lipido at his side, Mr. Ormsby
walked forward to stand behind Commander Sudcliffe, who seemed to be talking to Mother. As
Mother spoke up Mr. Ormsby was aware, as he had
been for some time, that Private Lipido was very
attentive to her. The boy had been impressed—as
had Mr. Ormsby—by Mother's going right into the
slums to bring Mrs. Dinardo, an old friend, to the
ceremony. The very image of fashion, nobody
would guess from looking at Mother that Mrs.
Dinardo really looked a sight. Like a weight lifter,

or something, now that he was closer to her and saw the size of the arm that held the parasol over her head. Really a sight—but there was Mother, pretty as you please beside her, and if anything a little proud of it.

At this point Mr. Ormsby was distracted by the silence, the complete silence, that followed Commander Sudcliffe's last remark. He had not really been listening—but now he leaned forward as Mother raised her hand and pushed a long bone hair pin into her hair. He knew that gesture so well that he winced, he *flinched,* until he remembered that this time it was not for him. This time it was for Commander Sudcliffe, and Mr. Ormsby peered at him, for the first time, with interest and sympathy.

"Am I to understand," said Mother, "that my friend, Mrs. Dinardo, is not to join me in the ceremony on the boat?"

"It is the custom," said Commander Sudcliffe, "that only one lady, the sponsor—"

Mr. Ormsby

"Commander Sudcliffe," said Mother, "did you bring Mrs. Dinardo all the way here to insult her at a time like this?"

"My dear Mrs. Ormsby—" said Commander Sudcliffe.

"Am I to understand," said Mother, "that a mother with four sons in the service is to be insulted by some silly custom you men have?"

"Mrs. Ormsby—" said Mrs. Sudcliffe, "the traditions of the sea require—"

"I have asked your husband," said Mother, "a very simple question. Does Mrs. Dinardo join me on the boat or not?"

"My dear Mrs. Ormsby—" said Commander Sudcliffe, and stopped to wipe his face. He turned to stare dumbly at Mr. Ormsby, who stared dumbly back.

"If there is not room on that boat," said Mother, "for a mother with four sons in the service—"

"Mrs. Ormsby," said Mrs. Dinardo, "now you go ahead—I don't care much for boats."

"Am I to understand," said Mother, "that my son Virgil fought and died so you silly men could keep a lady off a boat?"

"My dear Mrs. Ormsby—" said Commander Sudcliffe.

"If there is not room on that boat," said Mother, "for a four star American mother, then there is not room for me!"

"*Viva!*" cried a voice, "*Viva!*" Mr. Ormsby could hardly believe his ears, or his eyes for that matter, that this shout had come from Private Lipido. He stood with his arms crossed on his chest, his eyes snapping, and with the look of man very much bigger than he was. As they all stared at him he said: "*Viva* Mrs. Ormsby—nuts to the Navy!" in a voice that might have been heard a block away. Then looking at Mr. Ormsby, he said: "It's all right —*viva* means for our side!" and inhaled deeply as if to shout it again. Everybody had heard it—but Mr. Ormsby could see that nobody believed it any more than he did—they just heard it, that's all.

"Before we leave—" said Mother, who did not

appear to have been interrupted, "I feel it my duty to say that I will not have my son's name on such a boat. I am also obliged to say that I will have to look into any custom that forbids an American mother to set foot on one of our ships."

"VIVA MRS. ORMSBY!" cried Private Lipido. "VIVA DINARDO—NUTS TO THE NAVY!" Some of the people who were seated stood up to see who was shouting like that, and Mr. Ormsby could feel the eyes of the crew on the back of his neck.

"If it were in my power—" said Commander Sudcliffe.

"Heavens!" said Mother, "I almost forgot—why I almost forgot that it isn't even your boat! You men!" she said, "why it isn't yours till I give it back!"

Commander Sudcliffe took off his hat, wiped the top of his head.

"Until I've done what I came here to do it's more my boat than anybody's! Warren!" she called.

"Here!" said Mr. Ormsby.

"Find me that letter!" said Mother, and Mr.

Ormsby took out the collection, stared at them. "While you're looking for it," said Mother, "Mrs. Dinardo and I will look at the boat. Young man," she said to Commander Sudcliffe, "how do ladies board my boat?"

Commander Sudcliffe started to speak, stopped, then stepped forward and offered Mother his arm. On her left was Mrs. Dinardo, and Mother herself walked in the shade, the parasol remaining over her head. At the ladder there was a discussion, as Mother insisted that Mrs. Dinardo, and Mrs. Dinardo insisted that Mother, go first. Mrs. Dinardo submitted, on the condition that Commander Sudcliffe, who would come last, should hold the parasol over Mother's head. In this happy order they reached the deck. There, Mrs. Dinardo hastily recovered her parasol, and returned to her place at Mother's side.

At this moment they were all distracted by the sound of a car skidding to a stop on the pier. From it, a little hurriedly, an elderly gentleman in a smart uniform stepped briskly out and started for the boat. As he did, some member of the crew, thinking the ceremony had started, stepped forward and shrilly piped the admiral. Hearing this, Commander Sudcliffe left Mother and Mrs. Dinardo and hurried to the ladder just as the admiral reached the deck. Clearly, there was neither the time nor the place, on such a small boat, for Commander Sudcliffe to explain what had occurred. There they all were, and there was nothing for Commander Sudcliffe to do but introduce the admiral to both of them. Mr. Ormsby thought he saw the admiral pause as he was presented to Mrs. Dinardo—as well any man might before such an armored Amazon. But if the admiral knew—as well he must—that the traditions of the sea had been shattered, he was a gentleman before he was an admiral. Graciously, he offered the ladies chairs, and had the foresight to place his foot on the leg of the chair on which Mrs. Dinardo came down. It held, however, and then the admiral was seen to bend low over Mrs. Dinardo to speak to her. But from the way she shook her head, and looked at her red and green parasol, it was clear that Mrs. Dinardo wanted it *up*. Up, up over Mother, who now that she was on the deck, before the whole world, was perfectly at her ease.

All of this had been done with such dispatch that Mr. Ormsby and Private Lipido had looked on, fascinated, from where they stood on the pier. They watched the admiral take his stand before the microphone, adjust his glasses, and unfold a paper from which he began to read:

For his heroism and courageous devotion to duty—

Mr. Ormsby knew the citation so well, he had read it so many times to Mother, that he followed it like a psalter reading at church. He closed his eyes, and perhaps he became more engrossed than he thought—and a little loud—for someone tapped on his shoulder. This was a lady with a powder-caked face and spots of rouge too high on her cheek-bones—and she wanted to ask if they wouldn't please sit down. Mr. Ormsby understood her well enough, but he was diverted for a moment by a tic that fluttered the bag beneath her left eye. In and out, in and out, it went, like the gill of a fish. Then she walked away, and he saw that in the confusion he had been standing—they had both been standing —before all the people on the pier. Too late to beg the lady's pardon, he followed Private Lipido toward the back, where there were still plenty of seats. There they sat down—just as the admiral had finished with his reading and one or two people, who didn't know better, began to applaud. They stopped immediately, however, when Mother turned to stare at them, and in the quiet the admiral was heard clearing his throat.

"It is customary," he said, "to hear at this time a word from the sponsor, but it is more than enough, more than words can express, to have her here—" He turned and bowed graciously to Mother, and then was about to proceed when some strong voice interrupted him. For a moment Mr. Ormsby failed to realize that the voice he heard was Mother, as it was quite different from the one he heard over the radio. Mother's voice always did carry, and although she was far from the microphone it came through as if she, and not the admiral, were standing there.

"Mr. Admiral—" they all heard her say, "I have come one hundred and thirty-five miles to say something, and I propose to say it."

Mr. Ormsby had the presence of mind to put his hand on Private Lipido, who was inhaling, and preparing to shout something. While the admiral stared at Commander Sudcliffe, and Commander Sudcliffe stared into space, Mother stood up and walked to the microphone. Seeing her there—out there on the deck without a tree to shade her—Mrs. Dinardo came forward with the parasol. It cast a pale green glow on Mother's rose lace yoke and kerchief, but a fine rosy look of health on her face. Although she was not at all a commanding woman, especially alongside Mrs. Dinardo, there was something about Mother that arrested the eye.

There was something—and as she stood there, at her ease beneath the parasol, a tug drifting down the river let go with two loud blasts. The plume of steam rose to obscure the view of the bridge, the towers of Manhattan, and for a brief moment the ceremony came to a halt. It gave everyone a start, even Mother, but Mr. Ormsby was transported, bodily it seemed, to another time, and a distant place. He was whisked, as on a magic carpet, to Yellowstone park. There he had stood, with his young bride at his side, waiting for Mother Nature —as Mother always called it—in the form of Old Faithful to show off. What he remembered was the waiting, the big sky and the waiting, and then suddenly, like the tugboat whistle, there had been that roaring white plume on the sky. An incredible sight, a great natural wonder, and while the mist drifted on the clear air a small boy had tugged at Mother's hand and spoken to her. . . .

"Yes, son—?" Mother had said, as she liked to be correct with impressionable children.

"Why does it *do* it?" the boy said.

"Why does it *do* it?" Mother had repeated, and looked at the spot where the mist was still drifting. She reflected, then she said: "Son, that's Mother

Nature—Mother Nature, that's all." And that had been all. Somehow, the boy had found it enough. That had been all there was to say about Old Faithful, and if anybody ever asked him about Mother—

"Consider the lilies—" he heard her say, and hearing this he opened his eyes, as the text was familiar, though the application was original. He reflected on this as Mother repeated: "Consider the Lilies of the field"—as she had found it wise to check every loudspeaking system. "They toil not, neither do they spin—" she continued, and the feeling grew in Mr. Ormsby that Mother was speaking, as it often turned out, to him, *personally*. When the opportune moment occurred, she was ready for it. "And yet I say unto you—" Mother went on, "that Solomon in all his glory was not arrayed like—like one of these." As his eyes were open, Mr. Ormsby saw Mother's right hand make a graceful gesture, including the admiral, the commander, and the smarter members of the crew. He closed his eyes, mercifully, and Mother continued: "Therefore, if God so clothe the grass of the field, which today is, and tomorrow is cast into the oven, shall he not much more clothe you, O ye of little faith?"

For years Mr. Ormsby had been troubled—men, as a rule, were apt to be troubled—with the connection between Mother's quotations and her text. He was not troubled now. It was clear that a sentence had been passed. He waited, as men waited in every age and in every clime, for the walls, of whatever kind, to come tumbling down. A hood of ominous silence, like a canvas sky, seemed to settle over the USS *Ormsby*, the lilies on the deck, as well as the grass of the field. Then it was suddenly broken by the hoarse voice of the boy.

"Here she comes!" he cried, "Here comes Mother!" and rose from his seat in such a manner that Mr. Ormsby, like a man on a springboard, rose with him. As they did, so did every man on the pier. As one man they rose together, some of them, like Mr. Ormsby, a little stunned, but all of them able, with the help of their wives, to get to their feet. Coming toward them, soberly, was Mother, her flanks protected by the U. S. Navy, with Mrs.

Myrtle Dinardo still in full charge of the sky. So they came, the flagship and the escort, passing in review, among others, Mr. Warren K. Ormsby and Private First Class Seymour Lipido. As men who knew what they knew, and felt no need to talk about it, they stood, as converted men should, piously in their pew. As the escort passed, Private Lipido, moved, as the young are, to say something, leaned to whisper in the old man's ear.

"She'll surprise you, won't she?" he said, and Mr. Warren K. Ormsby allowed it was true.